MW01115491

Wild Hearted

Cover Design: Alexandria Zech
Book Design: Adam Donshik
Wild Hearted / Jesse Gros. – 1st ed.

ISBN: 978-0-9897093-3-0

For Dalai Mama

DEDICATION

This book is dedicated to the courageous members of the Wild Hearted Writers' Circle–People from all different walks of life who put pen to paper over and over, in the face of doubt and often relentless inner demons, to find their voices and discover that indeed: "We are Writers!"

INTRODUCTION

Dear Friends, come take a walk on the wild side and join us on an unexpected journey . . . .

Inside these pages are stories that will make you laugh, cry and perhaps provide clues to some of life's lingering questions. Most of this book was written in class by people who initially did not consider themselves to be writers.

The stories and poems in this book can be liberating and are sometimes intimidating. Don't let that stop you. Read slowly, take it all in, and enjoy the journey.

WRITE YOURSELF FREE

So often we suffer because we don't have the words to describe how we are feeling and have a hard time constructing an accurate story of our lives. We are confused by our paradoxical nature. One part of us says, "turn right," while another says, "go left!" We struggle to be present.

Once we are able to put our feelings and experiences into words, or someone else does it for us, it all starts to make sense. Their words heal us in a way that we have not been able to do for ourselves. In that moment, we no longer feel alone and our life comes into clear view. Self-compassion and forgiveness come naturally. Our separation from ourselves and others ends.

WHAT PEOPLE ARE SAYING

"This book is a treasure trove of personal stories that will leave you with a deeper appreciation for our collective human experience. The humor, wit, and grit in 'Wild Hearted' are a testament to the power of storytelling. What I love about this book is the fact that these stories are brought to life by people who had never before considered themselves writers. It's a beautiful reminder that each of us carries a story worth sharing."

Lynsey Dyer, Professional Skier

"Wild Hearted" contains ninety-five personal adventures and introspections into men and women writing, not talking, about their most intimate and motivating beliefs, goals, and challenges. When you write, it remains on the page rather than becoming one with the wind. Writing is hard work. But very rewarding work. You will appreciate that even more once you have spent private time with people like yourself who dare to lay it all out in black and white. Perhaps you will be inspired to do the same."

Peter G. Engler
Author/Editor/Publisher/Coach

"My gut intuition tells me that you're gonna love Wild Hearted! With authenticity, rawness, and open-hearted courage, the diverse voices contained herein explore the profound themes of love, loss, God, shame, adventure, joy, hope, and redemption. Take your time digesting and assimilating the words contained within Wild Hearted. They will certainly leave an impression!"

Vincent Pedre, MD
Bestselling author of *The GutSMART Protocol* and *HAPPY GUT*

WE HAVE COME TO BE DANCED

JEWEL MATHIESON

We have come to be danced
Not the pretty dance
Not the pretty, pretty, pick me, pick me dance
But the claw our way back into the belly
Of the sacred, sensual animal dance
The unhinged, unplugged, cat-is-out-of-its-box dance
The holding the precious moment in the palms
Of our hands and feet dance

We have come to be danced
Not the jiffy booby, shake your booty for him dance
but the wring the sadness from our skin dance
The blow the chip off our shoulder dance
The slap the apology from our posture dance

We have come to be danced
Not the monkey-see, monkey-do dance
One two dance like you
One two three, dance like me dance
but the grave robber, tomb-stalker
Tearing scabs and scars open dance
The rub the rhythm raw against our soul dance

We have come to be danced
Not the nice, invisible, self-conscious shuffle
But the matted hair flying, voodoo mama
Shaman shakin' ancient bones dance
The strip us from our casings, return our wings
Sharpen our claws and tongues dance

The shed dead cells and slip into
The luminous skin of love dance

We have come to be danced
Not the hold our breath and wallow in the shallow end of the floor dance
But the meeting of the trinity, the body breath and beat dance
The shout hallelujah from the top of our thighs dance
The Mother may I?
Yes, you may take 10 giant leaps dance
The Olly Olly oxen free dance
The everyone can come to our heaven dance

We have come to be danced
Where the kingdoms collide
In the cathedral of flesh
To burn back into the light
To unravel, to play, to fly, to pray
To root in skin sanctuary
We have come to be danced
We have come

TABLE OF CONTENTS

"THERE IS A WAY IN WHICH WE SHOULD BE EATEN BY LIFE... THAT WE SHOULD BE ABSOLUTELY CONSUMED BY IT. THERE IS NOTHING WORSE THAN GETTING TO YOUR DEATHBED AND FINDING THAT YOU HAVE BEEN GUMMED TO DEATH! AND YOU HAVE NEVER BEEN ABLE TO GIVE YOURSELF OVER TO THE TEETH OF EXISTENCE."

— David Whyte

CHAPTER 1

Life

BECAUSE... YOUR OWN LIFE IS A FIERCE THING TO FOLLOW

ASTRID VINEYARD HERBICH

We don't get to just walk gently into the dark night.

No, first we must walk fiercely in the light.

Life asks a lot of us.

It asks us to get up, learn how to walk, stumble, fall.

Trust, brush off, get up again and stand tall.

We crumble, bend and break

and learn to put ourselves back together again.

Life's love is fierce and full,

It wants everything for us:

Joy, pain, love, lust, desire, despair,

Passion and compassion, motion and stillness,

hurt and healing, it's all in the same touch.

Life wants it all and gives it all and takes it all.

And we, little boats, toss and tumble, float adrift for a while, or catch a stiff breeze

and go for the ride of our lives, screaming for joy, for pain.

For fear or frustration.

It really doesn't matter because life loves it all.

What a courageous act of trust it is,

To throw our little souls into the currents of life's vast oceans.

We can never know where we'll end up, who we will end up with,

Or who we might end up being.

We just row, row, row our boats, desperately trying to steer,

To give our lives some direction.

And maybe to some degree we succeed, we find the Northern Star.

And still, we end up in America instead of India.

And we shrug, and take it all in, and take it from there.

Because hey, that's life.

And it's intense and fierce and beautiful and surprising,
and mind-bogglingly mundane, predictable and
boring, it ebbs, and it flows and raves and calms
and calls to us:
Just do it, jump in, swim, float, let the currents carry you away!
To unknown territories,
Lost lands and loves,
New worlds of wonder and terror, or home where you belong.
Through fog and disillusion into unexpected clarity.
And then one day,
When you're good and lost,
You may stumble upon yourself.
Sitting alone in the desert,
In all your beauty and wisdom.
Take a rest then. Have a seat, have some tea. And sit with yourself.
But don't get too comfortable.
This is life we're talking about after all.
You think you know it all now?

Listen closely and you will hear life laugh out loud.
Look closely and you can watch the fog creep back in.
Just watch the world grip your attention and wrestle it out of your hands
with barely an effort.
And off we go again.
Swept away and under and head over heels, being put through the next spin
cycle.
Well, I intend to enjoy this one.
Let it toss me around,
Surrender to the madness,
Squeal for joy, go with the flow,
And maybe, just maybe, I'll come out squeaky clean on the other side.
A little wrinkled and drenched,
But happy and dizzy
And busted out of my mind and the illusion that I can or need to control any
of this.
Somebody is running this show, but it sure as heck isn't me.
I just bought a ticket and waited for the show to start.

Only to find myself standing onstage, completely naked, without any lines, bright lights blinding my eyes.
And someone offstage fiercely whispering:
"Go on! Improvise!"

MY BEAUTIFUL CONSPIRACY 2.0
JESSE GROS

To conspire in its root form literally means "to breathe together." That's a thing I do for a living: I gather people to breathe together, in rooms, in homes, under the trees. Together, we gather to breathe. *In-in-out. In-in-out.* "Breathe in love, breathe out stress, breathe in love, breathe out hate. Breathe in love. . . ."

With each breath, we draw in the most basic ingredient of life: oxygen. With each breath, we draw in hope. We breathe out stress, anger, sadness, tightness and psychic assaults on our energy field. Emotional assaults, auditory assaults – we deal with these things every day as they come to invade our space, to rattle our inner sanctuary on a cellular level. Millions of charged electrons smash into other electrons. We can no longer feel where our bodies end and the universe begins.

My beautiful conspiracy is to prove to myself that this life can be well-lived without all the fear, stress and competition that is beset upon us daily. What if we could live a life fueled by love, creativity, connection, and togetherness? What if the lie of scarcity is just that, a lie?

I conspire with the memories of my childhood to bring back the freedom of expression I had as a child. I conspire with my dreams to create a space for my daughter to dream and play as I have done.

My dreams are radical dreams, subverting narratives of againstness. US VS THEM. Or even more insidious, "auto-againstness." ME VS ME: I am not enough, I am not worthy, I am not "x" enough, I am not "y" enough. I should go buy some shit to make myself feel better. Tell me what to buy: Maybe a new car? Maybe a new face? Maybe get a new tattoo or two?

Peace is the cessation of againstness. I don't want to live my life *against* things. I am FOR beautiful things. I conspire with myself, with nature, with god, with love, with my creative muse. I breathe together with these parts of myself to become an engine for good in the world.

But self-righteous indignation is a juicy, delicious, and powerful source of motivation. The part of me that loves the struggle of GOOD VS EVIL is the same part of me that dines on againstness for breakfast, lunch and dinner.

It is my beautiful conspiracy to live a life of meaning and purpose, as close to my truth as possible, honoring both light and darkness, following my muse to the edge of oblivion and back. Sometimes it feels like the mantras of our society perforate my eardrums. Sometimes my own inner monologue is a potent producer of thought pollution, pumping out toxic clouds of doubt and self-loathing. Sometimes, I conspire with my higher self. I use forgiveness, self-affirmation and self-compassion to break my Ego's grip on me.

Just let me be.

WALK WITH ME
SARA FALUGO

So, if you walk with me
I can't promise that I won't start running
And if you walk with me
You can probably expect that I may just need to sit down
From time to time
Rest under a big oak tree
Lay my body on the tall green grass
Feel the earthworms aerating the dirt beneath my heavy limbs

If you walk with me
We will probably stumble across a few thousand butterflies
And accidentally walk through a pride of half-sleeping lions
And ride a freight train across the
corn-filled plains of the Wild West
If you walk with me
We will likely land in a paradise lost to the drunken wayfarers and to the
businessmen in their five-thousand-dollar suits

How many flavors of ice cream have you tasted
If you walk with me
We will definitely taste a few more
And a few more after that

If you walk with me
As you say, you will
We might just discover the secrets to the mystery
of the existence of love
of death and birth
of longing and desire

If you walk with me
I will definitely hold your hand
Lift you up
Clean off your wings
And guide you to clean waters

If you walk with me
There's a pretty good chance that we will soar through the cosmos on a beam
of light
fueled by nothing but love
If you walk with me
I will surely die
Only to be reborn again
I like to put on a new costume from time to time
And I'm perfectly comfortable with reinventing the wheel
I've even been known to jump off from time to time
Time
Jumping off of time itself
Landing in an ocean of bliss-coated peace
Like soft serve ice cream with a hard chocolate shell

If you walk with me
We will play charades
I will jump around making silly shapes and sounds and you can remind me
of who I really am
After I'm tired of pretending

If you walk with me
We will make love
But not the kind in storybooks
Or in the cheap rags hanging on the walls of the 7-Eleven
We will make love to the masses

To the lost
The lonely
The hungry
The disenfranchised

We will make love like a mama bird feeds her young
and then pushes them out of the nest!
If you walk with me
Like you've said you will
You'll always have a heart
to take refuge in
You'll always have a fire to keep you warm
And we
Will learn
to know
the true meaning
of home

TUMBLING INTO FAITH

ANJ BEE

I am an artist; I am a tumbleweed. It takes courage to be either, or madness to be both. Both exist in a land where faith is a daily verb. Both flow through life on inspiration, absorbing, feeling, and soaring through the world. I have always been a tumbleweed. As a child, I chased them down empty Albuquerque roads amidst the desert windstorms, enthralled by their meandering airiness, and yet their uncanny ability to destroy cars that foolishly attempted to drive over them. That was power! To be indestructible and still float on the lightest gust of wind.

Yet, I constrained that wildness. I traded freedom for a financially-secure gravity blanket to legitimize myself to myself. I weighed myself down into a motionless state, and my glasses-wearing alter ego was born. Let's call her Julie; as flavorless and unrecognizable as the bastardized Indian food the English created... safe and lovely, with a spicy soul locked at home.

But no tumbleweed can remain chained to a construct where the breeze doesn't flow. Here I stand on the ledge of change, left hand grasping the familiar branch of control, right hand grasping for a future it can't yet feel. Perhaps I should just leap and unleash myself on those open desert roads again, leaving behind the vile insecurities and ego-driven expectations that suffocate my creative spirit.

Creativity is an act of faith, and I've never had the faith in myself to finish. So many half-written stories that come alive in my dreams. So many unfinished paintings sitting in moldy storage units. Corporate success is always safer, for it is devoid of faith and vulnerability; it buries it.

But I'm a tumbleweed! ... aren't I? I reveled in the wild intuitive decisions, revolutions, refugee camps, Goan eco-villages, while continuing to hit the "defer" button on my graduate school acceptance letters... until I didn't. Then,

I buried myself under a mountain of "shoulds." Ever since then, Julie dressed in the morning, left my soul at home, and entered an office where I merely survived till I could return home.

Slowly, over time, you forget your soul is waiting at home. Slowly you forget how it feels to move through the world with magic pulsing through your veins. Slowly you forget the sensation of dancing in the rain.

Survival strips the sacred from life.

How could we possibly smile at the magic that surrounds us in each waking moment when we're enduring the grueling demands of survival? Still, I cling to that familiar branch that secures my safety even as it burns my hand.

I should send those wildly insecure, territorial bullies a thank-you card for driving me to the crossroads before I wasted years of my life silencing my soul. And now I'm perched upon the ledge – I look down into the dark abyss, to the left, then the right – still refusing to leap and secretly hoping to find another branch. I'm left suspended in time where every breath, creaking branch, and gust of wind is magnified by the stillness.

But the branch of security always snaps, despite our best efforts to prevent it, and we tumble anyway, or fly if we choose. What is the difference between tumbling and flying but perception, and perhaps a few minor scrapes and bruises? Maybe it's time to leap off this ledge and fly into the future that was always mine.

I am an artist.

I am a tumbleweed.

Finally – I'm not afraid to be both.

SEEN/UNSEEN
ARMINDA LINDSAY

Seen: the tears I can't not cry whenever I speak my brother Peter's name.
Unseen: the clinch that tightens around my throat with my tears' falling.
Is this a cause and effect? or is it simply Grief's calling card?

Seen: their 59th anniversary prompt on today's calendar.
Unseen: the lump I swallow around, thinking if I swallow hard enough I won't cry.
Is this going to happen every March 14 until I, too, am not here to swallow?

Seen: me hugging my almost 25-year-old daughter so hard.
Unseen: the internal argument I'm having with myself because I no longer have her all to and by myself.
Will I ever learn to share what is definitely my most precious thing ever? Do I have to?

Seen: the most amazing man loving me, walking with me and holding my hand all night long, every single night.
Unseen: the terrorizing thought gripping my chest that he will leave.
Do trauma triggers and PTSD ever go away?

Seen: shelves upon shelves of books behind and around me.
Unseen: my fear that I'm not smart enough yet, so I rage-read to rack up more volumes finished.
There's a reason I set a limit of 52 books per year. Maybe this year I'll not exceed it. Not likely.

Seen: me holding the microphone and singing loudly, "Maybe This Time," and "I Feel Lucky" in front of the room.
Unseen: my pounding heart that's not pounding so heavy, it blocks my throat

like before and before and before that.

I hear myself as I open my mouth, like there's an Oreo sitting on my tongue. Just like that.

Seen: my friend is sad and says it's hard for him to be with himself.

Unseen: my immediate walk back in time, to all the times I struggled to be with myself, too.

That journey is hard and lonely. I know. And I know it will transform you. You will Become, just like the Skin Horse. And just like me.

Seen: documentaries, podcasts (heard) and news stories about Mormons, Fundamentalists, origin stories and current events.

Unseen: the weight of my emotional separation from my family and their rights, their wrongs, their moralities.

Who can ever say when the crushing wound will happen to you? Or how it will splay you open, exposed and vulnerable to the man behind the curtain. . . .

Seen: me living my best life, finally.

Unseen: me living my best life, finally.

Can I bottle this up and stock my own shelves with it? Self-Preservation is the gift that keeps on giving me my Life.

"ISN'T FALLING IN LOVE ALWAYS RECKLESS?
EQUALLY THE MOST MUNDANE AND MAGICAL THING IN THE WORLD."

— Astrid Vineyard Herbich

CHAPTER 2

Love

I DIDN'T EXPECT IT TO FEEL THAT WAY

JESSICA ARONOFF

I agreed to go on a second date, not because I wanted to, but because I wanted to demonstrate – to myself – that I am, in fact, living into my daily mantra: *May I be open. May I be curious.*

He had been nice enough, good-looking enough, smart enough, engaging enough on that first date – more like a sort-of date. He hadn't been quite funny enough, but maybe my bar is too high on that front? Or maybe it – midday coffee at the golf course sports bar – wasn't the right setting.

So I went out again. Shook off the dread – perhaps too strong a word, but just a little too strong. I got dressed and looked pretty cute, I think, and went out on the date.

I didn't expect it to feel that way. It felt like. . . nothing. Pleasant, I guess. Certainly not unpleasant. Not uncomfortable either. The conversation was easy enough. I looked at him and thought: He's handsome. Good hair. (And that's hard to find in the 50-something set.)

And, still, I felt nothing. Not even disappointment. Not frustration. And definitely not desire.

One drink and it was time to go home. Good night. Thank you, I had a nice time. An awkward hug next to my parked car. He walked away, headed home on foot in the same direction I was driving. I didn't offer him a ride. I saw him bundled up under his down jacket as he walked, and I drove past, listening to a podcast in the comfortable and warm solitude of my car. I didn't look back.

I didn't expect to feel this way – knowing I am whole, even when I am alone. Even on Valentine's Day. I did know I could take care of myself, be self-sufficient, power through and be okay. I never doubted that – or maybe almost never.

But I didn't know it would ever feel this way: peaceful, solid, strong, clear, unashamed. I didn't know I could love myself into safety. I still forget sometimes. But I remember at least 51 percent of the time, probably even more.

I thought I had to grasp, hold on tight, shrink myself, contort, hide, dampen my light. But I am light.

I thought it was dangerous to want, need, desire. That would make me too much for anyone to want to hold.

Speaking my truth was not safe, I thought. Stifle until it bubbles over into anger… and then stifle some more. Anger definitely wasn't safe. Anger is loss of control. And control is safety.

Or is it? Life is telling me otherwise. Love is showing me otherwise.

I didn't expect it to feel that way: Free. Honest. True. Self-loving.

It was unexpected: Like laughing so hard that snot flies out of my nose. Like crying at the vulnerably awkward (and meant to be comedic) dance under the closing credits of the TV show. Like coming out of the shower to find my teenage son waiting in my room to snuggle, just because. Unexpected, like a rainbow over the 99¢ Store.

LOVE AND MIRACLES
ASTRID VINEYARD HERBICH

Miracles and love.
The things that put us together
And keep our particles from drifting off into space
And back into nothingness.
Life. Love. Miracles. Mysteries.
Love is a miracle and most definitely a mystery.
Why do our hearts open to some
But not others?
Why do stomachs flutter, tongues falter, pulses quicken, breaths catch,
Eyes turn to windows into the soul.
Why do we recognize kindred spirits, hearts singing the same tune,
Bodies easily moving into dance, inner light shining bright as day,
Visible like a beacon in the night.

Life is full of miracles.
But love may be the biggest of all.
Or maybe it's the most mundane,
Since that's the only thing we all really want in life?
To feel loved,
To feel safe and held and seen for all we are.
Known to the very bottom of our souls.
Even while desperately trying to hide how fragile and vulnerable we are.

People are like precious stones: Each unique and priceless, created under
immense pressure, and when exposed to light, dazzling and sparkling, flawed,
Magical and full of mystery.
Maybe that's all love actually is,
The opening of eyes and hearts
To another being's beauty and preciousness.
Rumi said:

"Love is the sea in which reason drowns."
Reason pointing out the thousands of ways in which
we are not good enough and not worthy of being loved,
Echoes of voices that made us feel ashamed of who we are,
Internalized and amplified in the empty, hollow caverns of our brains.
Flying around like bats, sucking our souls dry, feasting on our fears.
Get out of the cave.
Walk toward the sea.
And drown yourself in love.
It may take your breath away. It may toss you about,
Shake you to the core.
Let it.
They say it's not love unless it hurts.
Because love is the antidote to numbness, it wakes up our senses,
Brings everything to life,
Up to the surface,
To be felt, tasted, smelled, opens our eyes
To all that is possible.
That's the miracle.
Just how full of life and love we can be.
How deeply we can enter the mystery, with open hearts
Embracing our vulnerability,
Discovering all our strength lies in our fragility.

Our willingness to let ourselves be broken, wide open,
Drowned in a sea of love,
Relieved of our reason,
hearts finally set free.

NAKED

MARTHA JEFFERS

So, I waited! I waited for the precise moment when he would step out of the plane and see me. A surprise encounter was not what he would expect. Hidden behind the column, I watched. I felt an energetic tenseness while waiting as if it were our first chance meeting! I waited for the moment he'd see me and then? I swallowed quietly, remembering stolen moments that gathered us in a state of sheer passion! He would be pleased, I reminded myself!

The days of mental preparation flickered by in my mind - timing, location, presence, attire, makeup, heels - yes, heels, important before all else. And now, here I was waiting, prepared and ready for the inevitable moment of a sweet encounter. My heart quickened!

I carefully scanned the crowd of people at the gate. I watched for familiar faces or someone who might be there to greet him. No one seemed familiar. The jet landed. My breathing became shallow as people disembarked from the aircraft. My knees felt weak. Am I prepared? Should I have stayed away? I stood behind the column, steadying myself, ensuring I was not revealing my secret. I waited nervously. My body filled with excitement; my head spun, wondering what he'd do. What would he say?

And then, the moment arrived when I saw him. . . I knew it was perfectly planned. My timing was perfect. He'd been gone for two weeks! We'd had but a few calls to connect, missing each other's touch, voice, and presence.

My heart skipped, hands in my coat pockets, I stepped out into the aisle, moving ever so slowly to meet his gaze. I stopped. He saw me. Eyes met. He stopped. At first, a look of surprise, then a faint smile of acknowledgement. He saw me. His look, penetrating. He moved slowly toward me as I met him. And then, with a sweep of his strong arm, he grabbed my waist and pulled me to him. No words were exchanged. In silence, we walked through the busy airport engulfed in our own sexual halo, breath still, wonder peaking around the corner of our unspoken desires. Me, standing 5-foot-1, in my long black winter coat and three-inch heels. He, a towering six foot three, in his casual Florida suit and sharp vintage canvas shoes.

We walked hand-in-hand toward baggage claim. Fingers intertwined, we spoke through touch – caressing the palm, tightening the grip, softening the grip as we walked. And still, no words crossed our lips.

He stopped. We caught our breath and faced each other. His arms wrapped around my waist and, with a gentle touch, his lips caressed mine. He looked at me again and, with a tilt of his head, questioned me with his eyes. "Could it be?" They seemed to say. He stepped back. With admiring and searching eyes, he surveyed me from head to toe! And then his face broke into a broad smile. Indeed, he recognized his prize.

He leaned into me and whispered in my ear, "I see your gift!" With that he swept me off my feet, twirled me around, and kissed me again slowly, as if savoring his special treat. More silence. I knew I had pleased him. I knew I had pleased myself, as I looked into his searching eyes. He grabbed my hand and we walked outside.

As if to test his curiosity, he slowly unbuttoned the top three buttons of my coat. His eyes widened. His mouth met my lips again. What awaited him was pure pleasure wrapped in a long black coat, a naked body perfumed in *Eternity* and vulnerably adorned in pearls, and those three-inch heels.

THIS HEART OF MINE
MICK BREITENSTEIN

I've worked diligently over the years to not have my past running the show in the present. And as all of us here are aware, that is oft-easier said than done. I've arrived at an interesting place. As a writer, actor, and creator, I've been able to use my experiences – the good, the bad, and the ugly – as a sort of painter's palette. The stories of my life provide the color and texture for me to create and share my craft. At times sadness and grief still arise. Old pains and scars itch and ache, but smirks and smiles come to visit in the present retelling of it all.

I was born a lover. I can clearly remember feeling the pangs of love as early as five years old. I can't remember her name. We were in kindergarten together and she had this cute almost bowl cut, the kind of haircut that Lego figures have, perfectly edged out around her ears. I didn't have many birthday parties or celebrations as a kid, but when my mom was still around, she threw a surprise 6th birthday for me.

As I walked out the door of the kitchen and into the backyard, I saw her... God, I wish I could remember her name. I wasn't psyched about the surprise party, but she made up for it in spades. I remember my heart was so full and my whole body felt warm. Everyone else could have disappeared in that moment and I would have been perfectly content with just the two of us. Five fucking years old and I was smitten!

We all, at one time or another, will experience "heartbreak," right? No one wants it. It's awful when it happens and it can be equally bad if you are the cause of someone else's heartbreak. My mother moved out of the house when I was eight, Scott was six, and Corey was five. That time is a blur and was so very confusing. Especially the mornings when we could sense the presence of a female in our parents' bedroom. Excitement stirred in us. We thought, "maybe Mom's home," only to discover it was one of the waitresses from the restaurant my dad ran. They were all very nice and sweet and usually very pretty.

Even more confusing when one of those times we felt that female presence and it actually was Mom in bed with Dad. I was too young to understand the subtleties and complex nature of divorce and relationships and clueless about how confused the adults in my life were. My mom was barely 30 and my dad was just a couple years older.

After a year of bouncing around efficiency apartments that were too small for 3 growing boys to sleep over, my mother decided to move to Florida. This was the late seventies. There were no cell phones or FaceTime calls. One weekly Sunday night call for 10 minutes each with Mom was all we got. I wouldn't see her for a couple of years. That was my first heartbreak.

Anyone falling in love at 5 years old may just be destined to experience heartbreak by the time they are 9. At least, that's the story I made up. In truth, I was angry, hurt, confused, and forced to navigate a completely motherless home. But don't worry, this is not a sob story, y'all.

I feel kind of fortunate to have experienced that kind of heartbreak so early in life. The heart is a muscle and the damage and tearing that mine experienced back then created the space for my heart to expand later in life. It took some time and a lot of soul-searching, shadow dancing, and mistakes to understand my heart. I raged for years. The internal pain was too great for me to interpret or integrate.

In those years, I built a wall around my chest. Building model airplanes and doing impersonations of the Temptations with my brothers gave way to kicking and punching. I beat the living hell out of my brothers anytime they disobeyed or disrespected me. I got into scraps on the school bus, at the bus stop, in school, after school, with friends, nemeses, older kids, and my dad. I was fighting my way out of sorrow and that journey to healing was brutal.

The steel trap that held my heart wasn't impenetrable. I allowed access whenever I came across sweet souls. I knew who was not to be trusted and became adept at determining who the assholes were. I quickly learned to surround myself with sweet, lovely people. That would be my way out of the grief and shame of my violent years.

This heart of mine has been beaten, bruised, and buried. Those years of protecting my heart had their merits as well. It was as if I was running through a minefield and it was necessary to build a structure around this most precious thing, this truest and most sacred part of my nature until I got to the other side.

These days, this heart of mine is expansive, strong, and free. I have an abundance of love in my life, almost too much (if that's possible). And you know what? I wouldn't change one goddamn thing.

DANCING WITH OUR WOUNDS
PAMELA HENRY

He menacingly lumbered down the hallway toward me with bloodlust in his eyes. Fear gripped me. *Did I truly believe he would kill me?* Before I could find out, our oldest son tackled him to the ground, thwarting his violent intentions. An act for which I was grateful and remorseful at the same time. An act no child should have to endure. That day, I told my ex he had to leave. I should have called the police, but I didn't, out of some misguided sense of loyalty. How had we gotten here after almost 30 years of marriage?

I see this moment through a very different lens now. I learned that my ex is what you would call a "covert narcissist." I am the empath his victim feelers sought out. Both of us experienced the prescribed lack of parental love and guidance as children to put us into our respective adult roles. It was a detrimentally-perfect relationship, like a parasite and its host.

As a child, I became an empath to survive in a household of functioning alcoholics. I have so much love for that young version of me. I honor her, but I don't have to be her anymore. Well, I guess I still am her, in some ways, but with more personal awareness. I am grateful that this troubled childhood and my gifts of survival allow me to tap into spiritual dimensions.

Without the breakup of my marriage and the breaking open of me, I wouldn't see and know these things. Am I ready to say I am 100% grateful to my ex for blowing everything up? Not really, not yet, but maybe I'm 50% ready. I'm still angry that he blamed me for everything. Deep down, I always knew our challenges were not completely my fault. But I ignored my intuition and let him project onto me everything he hated about himself. It was classic narcissist/empath stuff. Now, I'm not implying that I was without fault here. I am fully aware of my shortcomings. I chose him, and he chose me. We danced together with our wounds, attempting to heal.

Could we have learned all the lessons we set out to teach each other sooner? It's hard to say. I know better than to judge myself for that. We are here to learn what we need to learn, in this lifetime or another.

IT WAS RECKLESS, FABULOUSLY RECKLESS

ASTRID VINEYARD HERBICH

Liberating, exhilarating,
Fantastically terrifying.
And yet such a small thing to do in the grand scheme of things.
Isn't falling in love always reckless?
Equally the most mundane and magical thing in the world.

It's reckless to fall in love.
And equally reckless to acknowledge having fallen out of love.
To leave a love behind and move on into a new life, a new self.

A self, shaped by this old love, with a heart altered to such a degree
That it just couldn't fit the mold of that old love anymore.

Reckless, this falling into and stumbling out of love.
This creating a life centered around another person only to watch yourself
take a wrecking-ball to it all.
I've crawled out of these demolition sites,
Brushed the dust off my body,
And walked away from potential lives several times now.

And now I find myself . . . not so reckless anymore.
Reluctant to build my life around someone else.
Reluctant to relinquish any aspect of the life I have created for myself,
for someone else's comfort.

I find it so difficult to trust.
To trust that we won't recklessly wreck it all.
I find I am tired. And maybe a little scared.
I am tired of rebuilding and reconstructing myself after having been torn
down.

I'm wary of love's ability to make you want to throw yourself into the fire and burn.
Wary of my heart's longing for that fire, knowing it already holds all my old, cremated loves within its depths.

While I feel stronger today than I ever have,
having learned to rely on my own resilience and strength,
and not lean on anyone else,
I think I've lost my recklessness somewhere in that last fire.

Maybe I had stored it in the same chest I kept my trust.
I think they both may have gone up in flames.
Or maybe I just misplaced them.
Lost in storage somewhere, in some forgotten, unlabeled box.

But I do remember what it was like to be reckless.
What it felt like to trust.

Maybe one day I'll go and see if I can find them again.

Because there is one thing I have never lost.

Hope.

DESERVABILITY
IONA RUSSELL

(My heart is beating loudly as I write this.)

Shhhh... Silently flipping thru the rickety – worn – out – golden – gilded – Rolodex of my heart.

Are you deserving of love?

Hmmm...

What is your worthiness – ability to deserve the pure diamond crown of the heart?

Of my heart? Of her heart? Of his heart?

Where have you creatively applied the pigmentation of your harlequin's golden glitter, like Wite-Out, masquerading as the virgin maiden, the harlot of Harlem, or the mother – of – oh – so – fucking – superior?

Are we not all created equal, birthed beautifully and majestically of the same painters' brush?

Are we not one of many faces, of many colours, many philosophies, and fantasies?

And does it not all ebb and flow, like the unique depth of your own particular castle moat on the shore of your defenses? Depending on your perception, be it from the balcony of the Emperor's Palace, pure and clean, or from the shadows in the slums of poverty, putrid and desperate to pay the piper a penny or two, the self-righteous – the pure-est, the ever-opposing realigning viewpoint.

Ooops, there it is: 'cancel culture,' there goes another one, there goes the ideal of what it is to love, to be loved, to be beautiful, to be hated, to be envied, to be looked up to. Does Disney paint your ideal and do you live up to it? Come on, really, REALLY. . . ??? Or did you get dealt a stinking hand by the devil of perception?

What colours do you see in your Rolodex of judgment and love, of misaligned entanglements, giving of yourself too soon, not soon enough, judgments passed with no evidence, just speculation?

Did you notice I said JUDGMENT? . . . quite purposefully, I will have you know.

Swoosh, flipping thru the Rolodex of my heart, it needs some oil on the hinges. It's had a slightly tarnished bumpy ride out there.

I shall share a secret with you, one I hold hidden in the silent yellowed pages of my too -much- too- soon- too -fast -too- far- out there - young adult self. I kept a list of all my fucking - misunderstood - miss-constructed - miss-takes and miss-haps… of my wild and brazen, misbegotten conquests.

Looking for love in all the wrong places, finding heartbreak, reflections of the very thing I wanted to avoid, like the hard burnt crust of decaying treacle, melting down and spoiling the sweet homemade lemon sorbet of innocent delight.
Does this shock you?
Do you judge me?
Ah, you see, I did hint at my use of the word JUDGMENT earlier, did I not?
Let he or she who has not sinned cast the first stone.
Is that you, my lovely?
Are you without sin, without judgment, without error as you have trodden this human life, trying to understand, wanting to fit in, and yet, also afraid? Oh, so very afraid to let love in…. Well, that was me. I built a big stone castle around my heart. And when all my friends were playing "when I grow up and get married," I was declaring, "when I grow up and get divorced!" Well, like a good Disney movie that wish, as all wishes do, came true, for I believed it to be so. And so, it was!

I'm jumping ahead… tarnished by relationships by the age of 8 after witnessing a bloody battle of divorce, deception, and lies of the HBO network kind. I swore I'd never let love in after I saw what it did to my mum.

And now you may wonder about that list of conquests, well that came later. I didn't start too young by some standards, but I am not sure of your own personal standards, so perhaps I did. And I still have it somewhere in those yellowed out - worn out - sold out lists… in an 1800s suitcase belonging to my grandmother when she was a child. (Oh, how she showed me unconditional love, and she is one of many who did, so don't shed a tear.)

A is for Andrew, my first boyfriend but not my first kiss… Age 14 I was still a virgin.

B is for Bitch as they claimed I was, as they tarred me in that small backward misbegotten town… I was still a virgin.

C is for Cherry popped too soon, but I'm not saying when.

D is for David my first love. I was 18 and thought I'd marry him, until he cheated on me. My radiant mother was worried and beside herself that I'd end up barefoot and pregnant in that smog-infested shit hole of a town.

E is for Every brick I added to that wall around my heart, or perhaps ESCAPE would be better here. But I had to add a brick or two, don't you see… for building castle walls.

F is Forever, a myth sold by Disney, and 80s sitcoms.

G is for Growth

H is Hallelujah

I could run thru the alphabet, I could share my list, but it might turn your luscious locks a whiter shade of pale.

Like all good songs, let's skip to the good bit. . . .

In a cheeky way, I found myself on many, many, MANY adventures and if truth be told, I'd not erase or eradicate any of them. I have loved, and I have laughed. I have jumped off the edge of the cliffs of reason. I have danced with the Joker and the fool, and I have led that dance into my own unfolding daydream delight of deservability. I have fulfilled my destiny, for I am here as a Divine expression of LOVE. L.O. V. E. LOVE.

Each step, each dance, every paint stroke.

Every drawn breath.

Every pigment of colour and imagination makes up this tapestry of peacefulness you see before you, for I have lived, and I am L. O. V. E.

And I am re-engaging with my dreams.

Are you?

LOVE IS LOUD
ARMINDA LINDSAY

Growing up in such a large family meant many things were certain:

1. There was never not noise and commotion.

2. If you wanted seconds, you had to hurry through your first serving.

3. Everyone shared a bedroom with at least one other person.

4. Gardening was how we fed ourselves and participation was not optional.

5. We all sat down together for supper every night.

6. Monday nights were reserved as family nights, no exceptions.

7. "Emergencies" like bleeding, broken bones or illness earned you focused and, often, immediate attention from 1-2 stretched-way-too-thin parents.

8. Bedtime was a three-ring circus operating precariously under the supervision of an always-distracted ringmaster.

9. Anytime the arguing got loud enough to draw the attention of a neutral party, said neutral party would start singing my parents' favorite song for just such an occasion: "There is beauty all around, when there's love at home. There is joy in every sound, when there's love at home," and their singing would be met with shouts of "SHUT UP!" from the arguing parties now being reminded that Love is not supposed to be so loud. But who wants to think about love when such injustices are being committed against you right here in the family room?

Loud. Love actually is loud sometimes. At least that's my experience in my family of ten. How could it ever be anything different than it was? Than it still is, even today, with all eight of us siblings grown with families of our own? We love out loud; it's what we know to do because our parents loved us out loud through every "Make your bed" reminder, "It's your turn to help with the dishes," warning, through Saturday mornings listening to Daddy singing *Old Man River* with his left arm draped on the open window of his 1976 red Ford pickup truck, while I sit quietly buckled into the middle seat feeling his bigger-than-life right arm bump against me every time he shifts gears, the steam escaping Mama's old iron waiting alongside the hum of her Singer sewing machine stitching my dreams-come-to-life dresses, after-dark-only games of *Ghost in the Graveyard* with Daddy as both ghost and protector (when his surprising roars scared you to tears), the turning of the front wheels against the gravel drive coming or going with yet another precious cargo driven by an exhausted chauffeur mother.

Love is loud.
I wouldn't hear it any other way.

UNDER THE TREE
PATRICK FAULWETTER

I realized that it is my heart's energy that drives my little universe. I never allowed myself to love. I always wanted to, but love was trapped in little boxes, in a maze of tall walls. It was hiding in the cracks, with tiny threads spilling out, like grass forcing its way through broken concrete.

Love always needed a reason. Love had to be justified. Love only made sense when it was serving some outcome, some goal. When my last relationship ended, it seemed like a failure, because it didn't lead to that white picket fence or "happily ever after."

Art has always been my lifeline. It is the one thing that was true to me and, at the same time, generated a wonderful income. Love expressed through art was always safe, as long as it was accepted in the marketplace. My love was bound by transactions, and I had put my art to work.

A wise man under the tree said, "we are all on overtime." What an ephemeral realization compared to the mechanistic rhythms of everyday life, with its goals, identities and 401k's. Under the tree I received a communication: it was time to set myself free.

For as long as I can remember, I have been afraid to love people. It felt dangerous. Love always seemed to lead into a maze of conditionality. I was afraid being too close to people would limit my art.

Under the tree it hit me – it's not true! *Love and art are the same thing*: fierce, raw energy that needs to be cultivated, trusted, and channeled. Joined together, no longer in opposition, like a powerful, pristine, river of truth, this force will ultimately carve a path for me right through the maze of my heart.

THE BEAUTY I SEE IN YOU

ASTRID VINEYARD HERBICH

The beauty I see in you, and me,
Is our daring to venture out into this crazy life,
knowing that our hearts will be broken.
That our egos will be shattered.
Our minds lost.
That indeed we will lose everything and everyone we have ever loved.
For we will die and leave it all behind.

I see the beauty of that.

I see the beauty of that in your sad eyes.
I feel the beauty of that in my broken heart.
I am awed by our courage as I see us stumbling blindly about.

Rumi said: *"You have to keep breaking your heart until it opens."*

You and I, we are a part of all that is created and then, with a child's gleeful laughter, obliterated and destroyed.

And I see the beauty in that.

I will keep falling in love with things, moments, people who make my soul sing, knowing that when I lose them, it will break my heart.

I will keep breaking my heart until it opens, until it feels, knows, learns, trusts, that underneath all that loss and destruction, lies something indestructible.

I see in you all the courage I lack.
I see in you all the wisdom I long for.
I see in you all the pain I refuse to feel.
I see in your beauty everything I've ever longed to be.

I see in you all the choices I haven't made.
I see in you all the choices I have been spared.
I see in you a version of myself that reminds me that I have to choose who I want to be.
I see in your eyes my own longing and loneliness.

I look at you and see an aspect of God that had been hidden to me until now.

Your beauty reminds me of my fragility.
Your frailty reminds me of my strength, as I help you to your feet.

I look at you and I see myself.
I look at myself and I see a stranger.
The light in me sees the light in you.

The darkness in me longs to hear about the darkness in you so that, together, we can shed a light on it.

Or maybe we'll just sit in darkness together, keeping each other company.

I will hold your hand for a while and witness your beauty.
For you are beautiful whether in shadow or light.

I will hold your hand and when you are ready to let go, I will let you go and witness how shadow and light caress your back as you gracefully move on.

And I will hold your beauty in my heart until the image fades and even shadow and light move on to play on someone else's face.
And I will witness the beauty of that moment, and hold it in all its fragility, in my courageous heart.

Until it breaks.

And I will keep breaking my heart.
And I will keep seeing the beauty.
And I will keep feeling the pain. And the joy.

Because the beauty I see in you and in me, and in a sunset,
in a baby and a bud, a bird in flight and the moon rising on the horizon,

Are worth breaking your heart over.

Again, and again and again.

*"MOST MEN LEAD LIVES OF
QUIET DESPERATION."*

– Henry David Thoreau

CHAPTER 3

These Men I Know

MEN I KNOW AND DON'T KNOW
JESSE GROS

These men I know.
They work hard.
They drink hard.
Being inside their heads,
I bet it would be hard.

Living inside their karma,
I bet it would be even harder

It's our German heritage.
Little compassion for the self.
Help others first.
Suffer.
Become narcissistic inside that suffering.
Lash out.
Others suffer.
Hard work and suffering.
Good times.

These women I know.
They work hard.
They have big feelings.
They have mixed dealings.

These other men I know.
And many men I don't know.
They don't want to grow up.
I get it.
I wanna be a Toy's "R" Us kid!
These men, I know,

They seem neutered to me.
Domesticated.

These men I know.
They are not violent.
They do not fight.
Maybe that is the problem.
Maybe we need to get the aggression out.

So much progress.
Modern men regress...
Under the weight of it all.

It helps to be tall.
More of us to chop down.
Before we hit the ground.

But these men I know.
They seem happy.
Mostly.
They don't complain.
Or maybe that's just part of the programming.

These men I know.
Do they get to be heroes?
Is there room for that?
Does it even matter?
Of fucking-course it does!

Every boy wants to be a hero.

THESE MEN I KNOW
ASTRID VINEYARD HERBICH

So many men I know don't know how to say:
"I don't know."
And the less they know themselves,
The more they pretend to know everything.

That's what my father literally used to say:
"I know everything."

But he didn't know how to say
I'm sorry.
Or, I was wrong.
Or, I love you.
Or, please forgive me.

The most important words in any language were unknown to him,
and to so many other men I have met along the way.
So many of them scared and scarred,
And they don't even seem to know that.

If someone doubts them, or challenges them,
Or God-forbid, corrects them,
It seems to inflict a near-mortal wound to them.
Or emasculates them.
And they immediately put the world right again
By putting you in your place, put you down,
So they can be the kings of the world again,
A world where they are always right and can control everything.
Generations of men afraid of their shadows and anyone who reminds them
of their fallibility.

Where does that come from?

When did we decide men have to have all the answers, solve all the problems and be able to move mountains, in order to feel like men?

I don't know.
I just know that this toxic view of masculinity has men around the world trying to keep women small and weak and dependent,
So they can feel strong and big and powerful.

What have we done?
And how can we undo it?
Men unafraid of femininity, within themselves and the women they love,
Are still as rare as unicorns.
And they are as precious and as beautiful.

As women are stepping into their power and becoming more whole by embodying both the feminine and masculine principle and learning how to balance them within themselves, so many men still seem to be in a state of shell shock.
Not knowing what that means for them and their masculinity.

Because all of a sudden, they have to be more than just masculine,
more than just Men.
They are asked to step out of their generationally-defined comfort zone and be
Everything they can possibly be.

Both strong and vulnerable.
To speak their truth and admit when they are wrong.
Sometimes leading, sometimes following,
Soft and hard and able to laugh at themselves,
Admitting when they're hurt,
Use their hands for healing,
offer a strong shoulder only when it's needed.
To ask for help and for what they want,
And give generously of themselves and their time.

If men and women can find a way to allow each other to be whole human beings,
Maybe we will remember how to be at peace with ourselves and one another.

And how to be One without having to cut ourselves in half.

THESE MEN

SARA FALUGO

These men I know
are busting through walls
removing obstacles
setting fire to the patriarchal bonds
that have suffocated humanity for so long.

These men I know
are suffering too
in the darkroom
behind the camera
on film.

They don't see what I see.
I see their luminescence
I see their lightning bug wings
I see their luminosity,
and I see how they not only light up a room
but hold it
with their gentle presence
with their connected and kind embrace
with their silence,
with their essence.

These men I know
are moving and shaking
the structures
that in theory
should be their foundation
and primary support.

These men I know,
I know
because I have shed the old lenses
and put on a new pair of primo night-vision goggles
that see through all the bullshit
that the media
the religious institutions
and the over-culture in general
have tried to sell us ever since Cinderella lost her shoe.

I don't need a prince
shrouded in wealth and authority
I don't need a King
a General
or a CEO to give me my self-worth,
or to make me feel safe at night.

These men I know
far surpass
the prescribed version
of what it means to be a man
and what women have been told
to want and expect
from one.
When I look into their hearts,
and gaze upon their hands
I see everything.
Everything.

I see the medicine they carry
the wisdom
the kindness
the generosity
the strength
I see cosmic warriors
who are willing to sail into a storm
when needed

who will stand up for their daughters
their sisters
their wives?

These men
who are not perfect
who fail sometimes
are willing to look into their perceived shortcomings
rather than play the game
of "I've got it all under control"
business man
religious man
political man
intellectual man
counter-cultural man.
Whatever the wrapping paper
it is all the same to me.

These men I know
seem to have found a way to step out
even if it oftentimes means sacrificing
how they are seen by the world
and the level of respect that they will receive.

These men I know
are holding a tremendous amount of light and space
for the collective healing
of our species
oftentimes behind the many women
who are bearing the torch of liberation
women who may not have always been able
to recognize or embrace
but are now
in these shifting times
acknowledging these men.

And,

it should be known
that it pains our sisterhood
as much as it pains you
my brothers
when we witness our sisters
mistaking the spiritual glitter
for gold.

And,
it should also be known
that we are waking up
more and more
each and every day
and seeing you
more clearly
growing more attuned to you vibrationally
as we grow
more attuned to the wisdom
within our own hearts.

And,
as the resonance grows
stronger and wider
fewer and fewer masqueraders
will be able to pull the wool
over our trusting eyes
while
more and more of us
will grow to see you
more clearly
more completely
as we all learn
how to come together
again.

In this new paradigm
under a new framework,
and we will learn to value the heart more

and learn to recognize the leeches
for what they are
and to keep our legs dry
when it is time to walk through the trenches.

These men I know
are a balm to my soul
as I traverse this schizophrenic universe
where we are taught as children
that violence is bad
and yet narcissistic children in men's bodies
are authorized to run the world.

Thank you, my brothers
for your sincerity
for your flaws
for your compassion
and for your fire
perhaps one day
I will be blessed
to journey with one of you
in a deeper
more intimate way
or perhaps
I will live the rest of my days
admiring you from afar
grateful for the families
that you are growing
and the communities
that you are building.

What is most important to my heart
is that each and every one of you
come to see your beauty
your radiance
your essence
clearly

fully
without filters
labels
or histories,
that you simply see
how beautiful
and necessary
you are
in this world
at this time.

And,
that you are able to recognize
that many of your father's words
about what it means to be a man
are simply not true.

We do not need another patriarch.
We do not need another power-monger.
We do not need another pseudo-enlightened spiritual teacher,
or another billionaire, for that matter.

What the world needs now
is you
thriving
healthy
happy
joyful
allowing yourselves
to be held and supported
just as you are supporting us
what the world needs now
is for all of our hearts
to be held with reverence
and for that vibration
to be reflected back to each one of us
as we look into each other's eyes.

EGG SHELL MAN
PATRICK FAULWETTER

I'm the man walking on eggshells,
always walking on eggshells.
The eggshells are tied to my feet. I feel them cracking at every step. That's
why I step so carefully. That's why I don't do anything without the utmost
consideration.
Is that where the joy went?

My world is the one I created,
a world which is built from eggshells,
a pyramid of champagne glasses, ready to tumble.
One world spoken too loudly, one step taken too boldly, one move taken, too
risky!

I am afraid. I have always been.
I fear the soil from which those eggshells grow.
I never touched the soil; I'm wearing my eggshell shoes and my eggshell suit,
so I don't have to. I've never gotten my hands or feet dirty.

But there are cracks everywhere.
I feel overwhelmed and inauthentic relating to the outside world, because
that is where I have to tread carefully. I don't want my fragile world to break
apart. I know this is not reality. It's just my story, my eggshell story. I attracted
a partner, who bought into the same story. Humpty Dumpty, we inhabited
our Faberge eggshell world for three years, feasting on paranoid delusions of
how easily everything could fall apart.

At times, it seems the fragile world in my mind is all there is. But there are
moments when I briefly come home. I step through that weathered wooden
door, overgrown by moss, into my hobbit home. I leave my mind and come
home to my body.

These brief visits, they feel like a guilty pleasure, something which has to be earned. Only when I have proven myself out in the cold, harsh world am I allowed to warm my hands in front of the fireplace.

I want to come home.

I want to rest.

I want to settle down in my hobbit home.

BIG BOB

MICK BREITENSTEIN

Lately, I have had a challenge getting my breath meditation to deepen. Not so much the experience, but the actual physical breath. It's like I don't have the stamina or the energy to move the breath deep into all the cells, nooks and crannies of myself. I'm moved to go slowly and to be gentle with myself. No need to indulge in the shame story of "doing it wrong."

As I lay here, I was once again aware of my lack of energy. When I was instructed to "take the breath deeper," I pushed through my shallow, restricted breathing pattern and suddenly, a wave of emotion rolled over me. Tears streamed down my cheeks. With minimal effort, I was again able to take my breath further, deeper and stronger. Unknown to me, grief was trapped inside me, draining my energy and limiting my breath. When it finally released, I felt cleansed, and thoughts of Big Bob occupied my mind.

He was there in my quiet visions, just as I remembered him, smiling, larger than life, a protector, kind and jovial. Big Bob, Robert Reynolds was family, well, not literally, but he was as close to family as a friend could get. He lived across the street from us with his wife Adele, daughter Laurie, and two sons, Bobby and Michael.

Bob was my father's closest friend. They both drove these old, 50s model pickup trucks, like the one on that TV show, Sanford and Son. I think Bob even painted that on the door of his truck at some point. Bob's pickup was a faded forest green. It had the rounded hood and bubbly wheel wells. My Dad had a fire engine red version with a big cow catcher on the front. My brothers and I were so embarrassed by this truck that when my dad would drive us to the elementary school on Saturday mornings to play basketball, we'd duck down under the dashboard as we drove through the center of town so that nobody would see us in it. I guess our fear was that we didn't want to be seen as rednecks. We weren't fully native, not by the standards of those days in this small mountain town.

Big Bob was fully native. His family had been in the Catskill Mountains for many generations. Even though my family could trace some of our roots for many generations in the area, we were carpetbaggers to the true natives. Well, not really, but there was (and still is) a hierarchy in the local clan and we all knew where we stood.

Big Bob was... well, he was big. Not fat, but large like a line-backer on a football team. He was also gentle, loving, and generous. I never really thought about him much. He was just always there. He was there for all of our birthdays. He was there when my parents would get into horrendous arguments. He'd hear the yelling and screaming from across the street and come over and calmly tell my dad to go take a drive and cool off. Then he'd sit at the table with my mom, drink a beer, smoke a cigarette, and make us all laugh.

He was my dad's best friend, but he always protected my mom. It was obvious how much he cared for her... so obvious that his wife's resentment of my mom was palpable. I was aware of this from a young age and it never felt inappropriate, something my mother still says to this day. It didn't feel romantic or sexual; he was just authentically a loving person. He loved my dad, and by association, he cared for and loved my mom and her offspring.

We felt safe with Big Bob. He was always where you needed him to be. At a young age, around five or so, I would have night terrors and sleep-walk. Allegedly, I'd go right out the front door, walk across the street and sit on the picnic table on Big Bob and Adele's back porch. Somehow Bob would find me in the wee hours of the night, bring me home and put me back to bed.

One time I woke up, I remember the night. It was summer and the crickets and frogs were harmonizing in the warm breeze. Big Bob came out and brought me into the house. We sat in the living room and watched an old western and ate Oreo cookies and milk in total silence. Bob always seemed so lively, happy, like a big adult cherub of a man. He loved to laugh, drink beer, and be the life of the party.

It was October 1983. I hadn't seen Bob in a few weeks. He had been sick and in the hospital. There wasn't a lot of disclosure or discussion about what was wrong with him. He was gone for weeks; it was odd not to see him for that long... the guy who we'd pass by on the school bus and as we walked home from the bus stop. He was a constant beacon of support in a childhood of chaos.

It was a Sunday, and I was riding my bike to church just a few blocks away. I wasn't loving church, but the Minister's son was a good friend of mine, and his dad was a great guy. We'd play football in their yard every Sunday after service. If going to church was the price to pay for a great football game and getting to hang out with Brian and Reverend Goh, it was worth it.

As I got my first couple of momentous pedals in on my bike, I saw Adele pull up in her car. She had a few hangers of Bob's uniforms that she'd just picked up from the dry cleaners. "Hi Adele," I called out. "Hey, Mickey," she responded. "How's Bob?" I asked. She had a big smile. "Good, he's home, just picked up his uniforms. He's going back to work tomorrow." "Ok," I said, "I'll come by after church to see him." "He'd love that," she replied.

I continued to pedal on for about a half a block or so and I heard a BOOM! It was clearly a gunshot, but in our rural area, it wasn't that odd to hear. Hunting season was coming up. Lots of people around would target practice nearby enough to hear an occasional gunshot or maybe Bobby Jr. or Michael were hunting squirrels in the woods nearby. I didn't think much of it.

I don't have a recollection of Rev. Goh's sermon that day, but I do remember sitting in their house after church, eating a sandwich. The phone rang. Mrs. Goh got off and said that my stepmother had just phoned and asked if I could stay with them for the rest of the day. She said there was an accident: Mr. Reynolds had died and it would be best for me to stay put. I didn't want to stay. I quickly and intuitively put together that his death and that gunshot were related events. I felt guilty for being able to remain in the Minister's home in peace while my family and my neighbors were all sitting amid the chaos.

I was used to chaos; it was as normal as sliding under the covers to bed each night. I was having chaos FOMO. I attempted to leave, but the Goh family being such sweet people, well, I didn't have the heart to put them through a scene. I could have easily gotten away from them. I could hear the sirens; I could feel the pain. I guess I should have been relieved that I was in this peaceful sanctuary of a loving Christian home. But I was frozen. I couldn't eat, speak or move. I just sat in silence for hours.

I rode my bike home as the sun was going down. As I came up my street, there was an eerie silence that blanketed the scene. No wind, no birds, the street was on lockdown. I entered our house. My brothers and father were all lying in bed like zombies. Total shell shock. Nobody told me what happened. It would be days before I learned that Big Bob shot himself in the heart with a shotgun in his son's bedroom. Or that my dad was pulled off the toilet and ran across the street in his boxers to find his lifelong friend bleeding out on the floor. We never spoke about it. Us kids were not permitted to attend the funeral, no counseling, not one fucking word.

To this very day, none of us have ever spoken about it.

LIVING BRAVELY
MOTTY KENIGSBERG

For many years, I dreamed of having an action-movie-kind of bravery. I would get a surge of excitement, clarity, and direction for my life that lasted a day or a couple of hours, and then it would all collapse back into confusion and anxiety. My reoccurring thought was, "the fighter in me must kick in," or things will not be ok.

I would push and try to force things to happen, over-and-over-again, until I had forgotten how to slow down, to trust, to just allow things to emerge. Recently, it occurred to me: all of this pushing and forcing was actually slowing me down. Still, I yearned to be brave in the ways I imagined I should be.

My grandfather lived through the Holocaust in his teen years. He was nearly killed twice.

The first time, he was on a train loaded with thousands of people from Hungary to Auschwitz to be executed. When the train arrived, after he saw the sign for Auschwitz, for an unknown reason, the train turned around, and took them back to Hungry.

The second time, he was in line to be shot at the Duna in Budapest. There were two SS soldiers walking a small group of Jewish men to the execution line. One of the soldiers told his fellow guard, "you can go get more. I got this guy." He walked away with my grandfather. Once they were far enough from the line, the soldier told my grandfather "*go!*" in Yiddish, wished him well and let my grandfather escape.

Listening to my grandfather's story, I always wondered if running away would be scarier than staying in line? If he ran, he knew they could shoot him in the back. And, by his own logic at the time, if he stayed in line, surely the soldiers would not kill them. Killing made no sense to him. Why would they kill him? What had he done to them?

Against his own logic, he ran...

My grandfather told me another story of how his brother-in-law, my great-uncle, was on a different train to Auschwitz. While the train waited in the station, he pulled off a panel from the carriage and crossed over the tracks to board a train going in the opposite direction. He survived. As a young child hearing these stories I thought, "this is how a man should live – bravely!"

As a young Jewish man, I inherited a relationship to courage built upon a life-and-death mindset. The inherited belief was: *I must push, push, push, or I will die.* Generations before me have summoned enormous amounts of courage.

In my life I don't need anywhere close to that kind of bravery to survive. *And yet, I know there is a place for me just as I am. A place without self-recrimination.*

I have learned there is more than one kind of bravery: the bravery of wartime and the bravery of peacetime. In wartime, we must fight and push. In peacetime, we have the opportunity to embrace the calm and create things without desperation. There's a time and a place for both. For thousands of years, my ancestors have fought bravely and survived. I am blessed to be given this life to practice the bravery of living.

"I DON'T BELIEVE GOOD AND EVIL EXIST. NEVER DID. NEVER WILL. NO ANGELS. NO DEMONS. ONLY FALLEN ANGELS AND WELL-MEANING DEMONS."

— Anonymous

CHAPTER 4

God & Stuff

APPEARANCES
ARMINDA LINDSAY

". . . because deconstructing a lifetime of religious dogma doesn't keep the lights on; outward appearances do."

I wasn't fine, even though my repeated spoken-out-loud words to anyone asking (most of all to myself because I'm the one who was questioning, doubting and struggling) were: *"I'm fine; I've got everything taken care of."*

I see her now through a different lens and my heart aches with her for how she hurt from the self-bifurcation of her outer and inner worlds.

Outer Appearances Checklist

— Single mom with her act together

— Daughter who's well-behaved, polite, well-dressed, intelligent, active in extracurricular, engaging, well-spoken, shines brightly/excels in at least two aspects of her life, appropriately downtrodden because of her absent father, yet remarkably strong and resilient because of her hands-on single mom who's got her act together

— Job that pays well enough to call it a career, thus negating the need to work a second or a third job to make ends meet, should also be "good at" and excelling in said position

— Home owner, pay your mortgage, keep it all neat and tidy, prepare home-cooked meals every single night, go ahead and start a food blog about that, bake goodies for the neighbors, walk the dog twice daily, volunteer to babysit the neighbors' newborn since you work from home (where it's neat and tidy with freshly-baked goodies)

— Go to church every Sunday, teach Sunday school, in fact, teach TWO classes because you're such a good teacher and prepare the best visual aids for your lessons, also wear sleeves at all times and no shorts or skirts above your knees — *modesty*, please remember it's your responsibility what other people think about you and your body and the obvious message you're communicating to the world about what you don't respect when anyone sees your cleavage, please also ensure your daughter is attending all her youth group meetings during the week, oh and there's another class we'd like you to teach daily. At 6am. Don't drink. No drugs, obviously. And most importantly, no sex for you, single mama. Nope, not outside of marriage. But you're welcome — and encouraged — to get married again. Let's not even discuss that divorce right now, shall we? No, of course not, but while we're on topic, why aren't you married yet? That must be **so** tough for you.

— All the usual adulting stuff you've got under control, yes? Taxes, dentist appointments (twice yearly), annual child checkups, annual Pap smears, are you having mammograms done yet? Please remember. Family get-together, call your mother, schedule play dates, grow yourself, learn to knit, read all the books, turn off the television, socialize, dance party for one?

My Inner Reality

Constant turbulence caused not by some fluffy white cumulonimbus cloud combination, but from a lifetime of religious conditioning juxtaposed with the revelation that I was quite certain I was definitely no longer in Kansas and the Oz in which I found myself awakening was as completely and entirely unfamiliar to me as wearing a sleeveless shirt in public without the literal ground opening up to swallow me whole.

Rumi said, *"The wound is where the light enters you,"* and 5 1/2 years of being abused by my husband left a wound large enough to fill it with a flashing neon OPEN FOR EXPLORATION sign that I have yet to turn off.

While I was busy exploring, excavating and reimagining God, I left my outward-facing light flashing *I'M FINE*, because deconstructing a lifetime of religious dogma doesn't keep the lights on; outward appearances do.

AN ANIMIST'S PRAYER

JESSE GROS

Nature is my Guru
Camping is my church
The ocean is my Jesus
The fish are his disciples
The mountains are my Buddha
The trees bow to his holiness, the Sun.
The animals feed on the fallen fruit of the masters.

I came from the dirt.
I shall return to the dirt.
There is nothing else.

All else lives in my imagination.

Or does it?

WHAT'S FAITH GOT TO DO WITH IT?

ASTRID VINEYARD HERBICH

This pen doesn't need me to believe in it to exist.
The tree outside my window doesn't need to believe in the wind,
To be moved.
I don't need to believe in oxygen to breathe.
I don't need to believe in the sun or the moon for them to find the horizon
And shed light onto my darkness.

What's faith got to do with it?

Why does God need a name, or a church, a symbol or a synagogue,
Priests, popes or props, decreed to be holy.

God doesn't need me to believe in him or her or them.

There is life flowing through my veins,
There is breath filling my lungs,
I am full of IT,
This "thing" that wants things to live, to grow, to thrive,
To change, to die and decay, to let go of form,
Just to find a new way to be alive again,
Rearranging my atoms into a new vessel for life.

If you believe you are alive,
Then you have faith.

If you've ever loved a person, plant, dog, painting or poem,
You've seen the face of God.

What's faith got to do with it?

There are books that will try to tell you
The story of God,
The glory of God,
The wrath of God.

But God is not a story to be told,
Not a thing mere words can hold.
No letters can shape her name,
No painting his face,
No doctrine their truth.

You can taste God's name on the tip of your lover's tongue.
In the sweetness of a summer-ripe strawberry.
You can smell God still lingering on a sleeping babe's head.

You can hear God's voice echoing in the stillness of a star-lit night,
The serenity of a sunrise,
The gentle hum of dragonflies.

You can taste God's love in your mother's/grandmother's/father's cooking.
Or a Christmas morning blueberry pancake breakfast.
Or a piece of fresh bread and cheese when sitting on a mountain top.

You can see God's face reflected on the calm surface of a lonely lake,
In the eyes of a true friend or true love, in your dog's adoring gaze.

God is everywhere.
To be tasted, smelled, seen, heard and touched.
Call it God,
Call it beauty,
Call it love, creativity or joy.

Call it what you want,
But open your senses to it and it is everywhere.

Even in our darkness,
Our loneliness,

Our despair,
It's still there,
Holding space,
Never going away,
Never leading us astray,
Watching us grow and grumble,
Prosper and procrastinate.

We honor God just by being alive,
By letting life live through us,
Flow through us,
Breathe souls into our bones.

We honor God by loving and honoring the life around us.
By acknowledging that all life is precious and holy,
Not to be killed, abused, tortured,
Not a mere resource, a means to our end.

We honor God by loving each other,
By seeing God in a stranger's face.
This hungry child is God.
This homeless man,
This raging woman,
This broken-winged bird,
My drunken uncle,
Your bitter mother,
A lost brother,
They are all God.

We are God.
Woven together by invisible threads
Into a cosmic tapestry
Teeming with galaxies, stars, moons and mysteries.

And together, we shape the face of God.

What's faith got to do with anything?

MY MOM IS COMING TO VISIT
LILIA SERAFINA

It's been almost five years since my mom has been to this coast – *the Left coast* – as my dad likes to say. The good news is, after a battle with stage 4, terminal Non-Hodgkin's Lymphoma, she is cancer-free!

Mom is coming to visit, and her visit is bringing up some powerful mixed feelings: anxious hope, self-protecting joy, and foreboding confidence.

I was there during the July 4th holiday of 2020; yep, smack dab in the middle of the pandemic. Our family decided it was time to reconnect, and my parents were asking, so we flew out. After a whirlwind of extended family outdoor barbequing, my mom finally paused and sat down with me for a glass of sweet tea. It was the first time she had stopped moving, cleaning, cooking, or exiting to do her "Keeping of the Hours" Prayers since I had been there. She sat down with me and I noticed a massive lump extending from the base of her neck near her collarbone. She had strategically covered it with a high, boat-neck tee that shifted out of place when she sat down. When I asked her what it was, she oh-so-casually called it "her goiter."

I'm not sure why my parents are so apprehensive about seeking regular medical attention. Perhaps it's because they've lost loved ones to misdiagnoses, incorrect prescribing of medicines, or seeing their friends suffer from over-prescribing. It was, however, glaringly obvious to me that this was no self-diagnosing matter, so I made sure she scheduled an appointment.

Everything went into hyper-drive after my mother's first appointment. Her treatment sprinted forward from the Primary Physician to the Oncologist, to an ultrasound, a PET scan, a CT scan, and finally a diagnosis, all within a matter of days. I was there with my two sisters and my father when the doctors prescribed my mother chemotherapy.

Hmm. . . my father.

I can only say that his body was there, but his capacity to handle this circumstance was not. He looked to me for guidance. Actually, he more or less acquiesced to me. He had never been much of a compassionate caregiver to my mother whenever she suffered from an illness or debilitating migraines. In fact, he loaded her into the front seat of a U-Haul with their 2-day-old newborn and drove 20 hours from New York to Savannah. When they arrived, my mom moved boxes and helped haul their furniture into their new house. And my dad didn't stop her. Yes, my mom was moving into a house, and unpacking boxes, all while nursing a 2-day-old newborn!

Now she was going through cancer, and the prognosis was one of the worst you can hear: terminal. I was the one who did the research, maintained the medical records and advocated for her. I took notes at every appointment and made sure the correct medicines and dosages were administered. Even the best-intentioned and most-qualified medical professionals make mistakes, and there were a multitude of errors that my overachiever, note-taking and borderline OCD attention-to-detail self, caught and corrected. (My entire family thinks I should have been a doctor.)

During my mom's chemotherapy, I remained for four additional months to care for her during the first three rounds, which are typically the most difficult. Then my aunt came to take over the last three.

Chemotherapy is no joke. It is sharply heart-wrenching to watch someone you love suffer and be in their most vulnerable state, both physically and mentally. All restraint, niceties, etiquette, and diplomacy fall to the wayside. What's left is raw, unfiltered humanity.

My mother's unfiltered state revealed many harsh truths. While I recognized she was in pain and grappling with her mortality, she told me she believed I was destined to perish in hell. It left me gutted. And not just hell... but a special place in hell reserved for people like me, "who are falsely directing people" away from her Catholic God.

The irony is, through my studies on Christianity, I've discovered a richness in spirituality that has inspired my own faith journey and created a more profound reverence for Catholicism and its spiritual disciplines.
But... My God is still not my mom's God.

Or at least, that's what she believes.

But this is my mom! My mommy, that I grew up with! The one who grew up with me! She was only 17 when she got pregnant with me.

She's the one that had a bastard child! She's the one that grew pot on a New York rooftop when it was illegal! She's the one who lived with my dad and didn't marry him until I was six years old. She is also the one who taught me about a loving God, a God who would always be there for me, a God of mercy, forgiveness, and who never breaks promises. She used to be fun! She used to be adventurous! She used to be hopeful. She used to dream...

Why would she be so judgmental of me?

Why would she stay with a man who cheated on her for all those years?

Why does she condemn in me, that which she does not condemn in herself?

Why does she believe God is so rigid now?

Why does she refuse to be vulnerable?

This week, my mom is coming to visit.

She's traveling quite a long distance to be with us.

I wonder if the distance between our hearts will remain?

GOD AND ME, WE HAVE HISTORY

MARTHA JEFFERS

God and I go back, as memory serves me, to the day of my First Communion. This was my first conscious encounter with the God whom my family worshiped. As a child, and as part of my Latin culture, Christ, the saints, and the Blessed Mother were the fabric of our existence. We said rosaries to the mother of all mothers, Mary. We recited prayers as petitions for a short stay in Purgatory after we died. We prayed for lost items only God could find. I remember witnessing my adored Abuela Rosa kneel in reverence at the cathedral and watched her lips move in silence like a popcorn popper rattling off novenas.

God was a Mystery. He was the patriarch, the assumed leader of the pack. As an eight-year-old, I knew him only by name, Papa Lindo. God was to be feared and revered, worshipped and respected. It was no surprise that on the day of my receiving my first communion, I was apprehensive and fear-filled. Would I be changed after the Host was placed on my tongue? Would I finally be worthy enough to receive God in my heart? It felt odd and strange at the time. I could not see him, feel him, or experience him. Like Santa Claus, I experienced God as the ever-imposing ethos of the adult world.

God was somewhere in the heavens. He was distant and not of this world. For years, I kept God at bay.

But then my babies came along at 32. The miracle of birth allowed me to feel a depth and quality of love never-before-experienced. The wonder of the child on my breast cracked my heart wide open. It was then when I felt the first stirring of a God nearer to my soul. We danced for a period of time. We navigated the swift currents of life for a while - me, asking for favors and he, silent, cool and reserved.

And then a breakthrough. It had to do with an entanglement of great proportions. A betrayal. On a particular day, a day when mountains were to crumble, I stopped at a red light on my way to somewhere and began to fervently pray for help. I prayed for a miracle-of-miracles. I prayed to Papa Lindo and began to cry.

With my eyes wide open, I sat clutching the steering wheel and waited for the light to turn green. Then all went quiet and time stood still. I was engulfed in a warm current of calm. The light turned green. I slowly moved forward. As I drove, I became fully aware that fear no longer sat next to me. My hands stopped shaking; my heart stopped thumping. The trajectory towards alienation I had experienced moments before had all but left me. In a matter of seconds, life took on a different hue. I knew in the depth of my being all would be well.

So, began a journey of building our relationship. It's been a journey of doubt, inquiry, and wonder, learning to trust myself and God in me. The journey has been paved with patience, tenderness, surrender, and most of all, love. The Divine "She" who embodies the humanness of who we are - all fractured and whole and complete - is the God that I now worship. Mother/Father God of all creation, Pachamama in all her beauty and fury.

The radiance of the Divine which was once outside me is now firmly embedded in my soul. The loving grace of all existence is matched with the conscious awareness that all is well. In the fires of life, the burning embers flicker God's monumental stirring for reconciliation. My heart is full! All is well. Me and God, we have so much history.

I'M STARTING A NEW CULT
JANELLE NELSON

Growing up, everything was Christian: Christian school, Christian friends, Christian music, Christian camps. Shoot, if there was Christian bread or toilet paper, my parents would have bought it. It was all very safe and familiar. I knew exactly what was expected of me and what my opinion was about everything, without ever having to think about it. If you had told me at the time that I was in the most widely-accepted cult there ever was, I would have prayed for you and your unbelieving soul.

Exiting was painful, and it took about a decade. To start thinking differently than literally every person I knew – who did I think I was? How could it be that EVERYONE was off? Mrs. Ellis, Erica, John and Diana, the Eastman's, my sweet Gramma. No, I had to be wrong. I didn't have enough faith. I had to be going down a "slippery slope," like the kind they warned me about.

I remember the day when the walls started to crumble. It was the day I started validating myself. I started thinking with my own heart and inner-knowing rather than my head.

As I look back, it was clear I needed a smack from a cosmic two-by-four to help me leave. Divine Source lovingly gave me the perfect medicine and I am forever grateful. The church where my then-husband and my dad were both pastors started to quickly unravel, and none of it was handled well. I was deeply-brainwashed in patriarchal Christianity and got to see behind the curtain of a prestigious, white, all male, elder board that was supposed to be "closest to God." Behind the curtain I discovered a bunch of wounded and unconscious little boys. My illusions were crushed and I was free.

After that wrecking and rebuilding, I started to allow myself to no longer be a second-class citizen. My intelligence mattered. My voice mattered. My opinions mattered. My intuition mattered. *I mattered.* I learned that even when we're wrong, we matter. Freedom is everyone's birthright, including respecting the freedom of those who choose to remain in the system.

I'm starting a new cult: the validating, living-and-breathing-your-own- truth, cult. Who wants in?

MY CEREMONIAL JOURNEY
MARTHA JEFFERS

Snuggled peacefully in the soft arms of what felt like a giant teddy bear, I gave myself permission to descend, permission to test the boundaries of my consciousness, to find a key I'd been searching for all my life. A key, I believed, would open the door to that place inside, that seemed eternally locked with no entry.

Something always felt missing. Something always felt incomplete. Something inside of me felt tightly wrapped and unapproachable. Certainly fear played its part. Don't we all feel a heightened alertness when we begin to peel back the curtain of our being? Afraid we might find a boogie man inside, or confront our misery, or worse yet, confront what we already know is true. We fail to fully admit to ourselves what needs to be acknowledged.

I've done a lot of internal work – scaled mountains of trapped emotions and met parts inside of me I had disowned. I've met myself in another and saw pain embedded in corners of my heart I thought I had healed. I've received feedback on blind spots in my personality. Through patience and great support, I've opened myself to the possibility of unfolding and slowly shrinking the jumbo ego I nurtured and strongly protected in the past. Yet, deep, deep inside, there was more to excavate, more answers to uncover, a key to unlock the "interior castle" profoundly described by Saint Teresa of Avila.

This night I slept a profound, quiet sleep while awake, wrapped in the warmth of a Peruvian blanket. The sweet oils of night-blooming jasmine deepened my softness, and I surrendered into the depths of the Divine. Through soft canals of thought, I journeyed and smiled at the absurdity of the moment. But in time, I was overcome by the absolute truth my soul had known for decades. The awareness did not come in the form of angels, fireworks, or even a cosmic explosion. No, the key appeared in the form of the Christ, the Jesus of my ancestral heritage: "I am your Guru," he said. The simplicity and clarity of the message were profound. My body received it and I felt a warm glow, like the early morning summer sun touching barren, exposed skin, kept cool under the night sky.

Jesus is my Guru, I whispered. The words seemed familiar yet of another language. They fell from my lips like liquid honey. There was no question or resistance or debate! It was so! I laughed and giggled like a small child opening a surprise box holding a new toy.

The ego fights the battle of separateness, but the soul seeks peace and oneness. The authentic self melds with the small self, creating expansion and inclusion of all. The key to our joy is our connection with our soul, our spirit, our Divine Indwelling.

In this precious moment in time, I breathed in a deep intimacy with the Beloved. On this night, filled with the scent of blooming jasmine and lavender oils, I found my key. As I melted into the arms of the One, I dropped the illusion of duality, the wrap of self-recrimination, and the cloak of misperceptions.

My night became ablaze with light, consumed in universal love. The fires of my ancestors ignited as I sang my songs and my Guru and I were restored to oneness!

DEEP IN THE FOREST OF MY SOUL

ARMINDA LINDSAY

The forest is dense, thickly-wooded and difficult to navigate, but not treacherous. Arduous and labor-intensive, yes. Dangerous, no. For many years I simply lived in this forest, unaware of the beauty and complexity of my own lush and vibrant surroundings, taking for granted all the natural resources residing here with me. I frequently took excursions lasting for long periods of time seeking wisdom, understanding, and tools for what felt like my own survival. The longest such journey I undertook was one on whose path I was placed, rather than a path I personally selected: the path of religion, of God, of my place of belonging amongst the other forests filling up Planet Surface alongside my own.

The long-buried secret no longer hidden from view is the return journey to mySelf I've been traveling these many years now, arriving at the truth buried at my birth: I am the wisdom, the understanding, and the tools I was always taught resided outside of me — that to be a seeker and a believer of God inherently meant the abdication of Self in exchange for service in His kingdom. That discipleship and devotion demanded I burn my own forest and call it faith.

What has been required of me is also that which I buried deep inside of me: all that I am, have, know, and do in someone else's name — giving not only all my talents, time and resources for the building, recruitment and regeneration of a man's kingdom, but doing so at my own Self's sacrifice, putting myself on the altar and striking the terminal wounds with my own hand, all while celebrating my dedication to the life of another's forest.

I traverse my own forest's floors, creating trail markers on my newly-forged pathways, certain I do not want to wander from these paths again, ensuring all arteries lead me back to mySelf, back to the truths I now know, understand,

and hold precious: I am the way, the truth and the light. I am the love I misunderstood was ever outside of me, was ever bigger than me, was embodied by a man holding a scepter of self-proclaimed power that I mistook for my personal proclamation.

My forest's secret teaches me that all paths lead to my own heart. My own heart houses and holds precious the truth of who I am and the strength of my own density is my gift and one I am no longer hiding.

I have unearthed this secret: I am the Love, the Light, the Way, and when I pursue these paths, others follow and find their own way, in their own heavily-wooded wanderings. We are all walking back home to ourselves, to the center of truth inside each of us and it's not a secret that should be kept silent. It's a secret I willingly declare and share.

Let me love you as I love me: with my whole soul.

"SHAME IS A SLIPPERY, SNEAKY DEVIL, HELLBENT ON SELF-PRESERVATION."

— Dr. Logan

CHAPTER 5

Shame

31 FLAVORS OF SHAME
ANJ BEE

A 5-tiered multi-flavor cake with potent colors and textures, a marble chocolate and vanilla underbelly, drizzled in sprinkles and candies of all glorious forms. A side of California-style churros with organic hazelnut chocolate sauce, or a side of the cream in rasmalai if that's your preference. Nauseatingly sweet, the perfect accompaniment for such an elaborate cake. Let's not forget some pistachio ice-cream or coconut milk, an elaborate and decadent accompaniment drizzled onto a multi-tiered vibrant cake celebrating the 31-flavours of shame.

But why stop there? Pick your whiskey accompaniment, as well – the smokey sedater, the dancing dictator, the manipulative magician, the peaty parrot – the parrot's squawking while reminding me of the shame echoing in my chest. My shame is so ornate, dancing deliciously before me, mocking the pain it produces in my body.

Shame is an omnipresent force, an ocean subsuming me since birth into its waves of different shapes and sizes:

> › The bottle of wine, the bottle of pills, and the bag of weed that were my mother's priorities; the religious devotion and technology that were my father's

> › The very presence of a South Asian kid who looked like a native American in a Christian school run by Mormons

> › The poor kid in school whose mother hadn't done their laundry in 2 weeks, who lay drunk in the small apartment that could've fit into her classmates' front-yard

> › The uncle who demanded I marry him and move to the Middle East – as if choice was only a construct that lived in a figment of my imagination

- Islam, Christianity, Sikhism and Hinduism, all demanding I pick their God, declaring I've betrayed my country, my people and my family if I don't swear thoughtless allegiance to them

- India and Pakistan demanding I choose one and declaring that I've betrayed my country, my people and family if I don't swear thoughtless allegiance to them

- Israel and Palestine, demanding I pick a side, each declaring that I've betrayed them and their people if I don't swear thoughtless allegiance to them

Shame is a multi-layered, vibrantly colorful, sweetly-nauseating cake that comes in 31 flavors.

But in my dreams I found the heartbeat of my shame. I reached into the hole of memories and dragged out the first suitcase, containing a scene from Roald Dahl's *The Witches*, being threatened to be burned at the stake for not abiding by their rules. Then the next suitcase, containing a sci-fi thriller in which the protagonist always dies by being stabbed in the stomach. Then the next suitcase, where the inner child leaps off the bridge and flies into the clouds. Then the next suitcase where the protagonist collapses from fatigue while trying to run through a labyrinth of trap doors. Until finally in the last suitcase: the source, the shock, the relief.

I danced with my shame, exploring how it moved, slinking and stinking through my universe, tentacles entrenched in every facet of my life and suffocating me into silence. Shame is pernicious. It is the great silencer.

I am tired of being suffocated by shame, a shame that surpasses the confines of theologically-based "original sin." It occupies the 31 flavors of intergenerational abuse, trauma, political violence, terrorist attacks, religious conflict, hummus-cooking conflicts, divorces, and to the very value placed on human life.

I am a radiant beacon of femininity that will forever have to dodge the arrows of shame that my culture, society, and family sling at me for not being one of them – for not fitting into one of their neat and tidy boxes.

CHOCOLATE-COVERED SHAME

ASTRID VINEYARD HERBICH

Some say we have a pain body.
A thing, an energy, that can be passed on
From person to person,
From generation to generation.
I think we do.

Mine feels rigid and brittle,
Like a hard caramel that will break your teeth
Should you try and take a bite of it.

I think I also have a shame body.
Passed on through my family tree,
Deeply-lodged within my roots, hidden somewhere in my DNA.

Because I remember feeling shame so acute,
In my tiny childhood body, it felt like a thousand small deaths.

Looking back, I have no explanation for its existence,
But it has always been there,
A thick layer of marshmallow mushiness,
Threatening to suffocate my heart,
Wrapped around my brittle pain like a blanket.

And then there is my vain body.
A shiny, perfect layer like chocolate,
Covering it all,
In an ill-fated attempt to hide all the mushiness,
And brittleness underneath the surface.

But apply just a little bit of pressure and it cracks.

Expose it to the sunlight,
Or let someone hold it just a little too long,
And it will melt.

And out pours all my shame,
And underneath the teeth-shattering pain,
And the whole thing falls apart.
And I don't even want to touch it,
Nor taste it,
Let alone eat it,
Even knowing the only way to get rid of it is to digest it.

That I SHOULD bite into it,
Let the bitter flavor hit my tongue,
Experience the texture and the temperature of it,
Letting it make its way through me,
Transforming it on the way,
And expel it from my body,
And finally let it go.

But rather I keep it in a pretty box with a bow
In the back of the refrigerator where it's cold and dark,
Like a precious thing
Someone gave me on my birthday.

The day I was born into the world,
Questioning whether I had a right to be here.
Learning to apologize for my existence.
After all, I did take up more space in my family.

Questioning whether I wanted to be here.
After all, everyone around me did feel so much pain,
And my little body soaked it all up like a sponge.

Questioning whether I was meant to be here.
After all, life did look so much nicer from up in the clouds,
Or deep inside a book, or song, or painting.

My pain, my shame, my vanity,
The bittersweet things better left untouched in the back of the refrigerator.

How long does it keep?
Does it ever expire?
What happens when it does?
I'm afraid it's a sugary time bomb,
Just waiting to explode in my face.

So now, I take it out sometimes.
Hold it in my hands; let the chocolate melt a bit,
Lick it off my fingers.

I take tiny bites of shame,
Shame of all different flavors, all artificial,
And I allow myself to taste it and take it in,
And let it move through me.
Not so much as to make me sick,
But just enough to slowly make my way
To the pain at the center of it all.

I don't know when I will get there.

To the place where I can take the brittle bitterness
Into my mouth and hold it there for as long as it takes for it to dissolve,
And let it move through my stomach,
My gut, my bloodstream, my heart,
And broken down,
Cleansed through my body,
Give it back to the earth
Where it can nourish new life

And turn into something beautiful.

ORIGINAL SIN, ORIGINAL BULLSHIT

JESSE GROS

I don't believe in original sin.
I believe in original innocence.

I don't believe that we are born sinners.
I don't believe that Gandhi went to hell because he chose to believe one story over another.

This idea of original sin seems to capitalize on the innate shame that so many of us feel from a very young age. A nameless, formless shame that fits neatly into the story of Adam and Eve. Sorry Steve, you were not invited to the party.

That's right, according to some very old books and the folks who follow those books, you and me, we were born with a stain and we will remain that way until we die. Then, and only then, if you chose the correct story, you get to fly free as a bird, absolved of your sins. BUT, if you did not choose the right book to believe, you do not pass GO, you do not collect $200, and you go right to soul jail for eternity.

Brilliant! Just brilliant! Using the sticky emotional leverage of shame, guilt and fear (in the booming voice of a late-night infomercial), "you too can control the masses! But wait, there's more!" Shame, guilt and fear can also be used to win elections, force compliance on social issues, and eliminate those who disagree with you. What fun!

No, not really.

What if it's all a lie? What if *Original Sin is* actually *Original Bullshit?*

What if all we are really trying to do is to get back to our innocence? What if the guilt and shame we feel are not actually ours, but gifted to us by life? Given to us by life events, trauma, and intergenerational family patterns.

Deep in a group meditation, one of my first mentors said, "If it's not LOVE, it's not yours. Just let it go." Tears flowed, gentle sobs filled the room and then – an explosion of laughter! A truth so obvious, when revealed, the only response was celebration!

So, what am I saying here? I'm proposing something quite blasphemous. I'm suggesting *there is nothing wrong with you* – no innate flaw or piece of corrupt code that needs to be fixed in this lifetime or the next.

"You are not a troubled guest on this earth,
you are not an accident amidst other accidents.
You were invited from another and greater night
than the one from which you have just emerged."
- David Whyte

I know this can be a hard one to swallow, especially if you have been feeding on the universal guilt trip that is foundational for many modern religions.

I remember the day it hit me, this truth: *There is nothing wrong with me.* No deep, un-cleansable shame that could only be expunged postmortem.

There is nothing wrong with me
There-is-nothing-wrong-with-me
There is nothing wrong with ME!
And the happy dance of self-awareness ensued. . . .

If what I say is true, then what is to be done about SHAME? Mucky, dark, and sticky, like beach tar between your toes, it stays hidden in our subconscious, passed on from one generation to the next, until someone (like you) stops the transmission. Until someone (like you) takes a stand to dissolve and extricate that dark cloud from our collective consciousness.

SHAME, SHAME GO AWAY
MARTHA JEFFERS

Rain washed over the earth these past few days, leaving behind the scent of wet grass, wet soil, and night-blooming jasmine. It also left the promise of a spring filled with bouquets of daisies, daffodils, tulips, and cactus flowers.

While staring out my window at the falling rain and listening to the thunder, I was brought to remember many of my past transgressions – the type that would have me beating my heart center with a closed fist while I repeated: "through my fault, through my fault, through my most grievous fault."

These recalled moments felt impaled and well-guarded within the structure of my being. I was so young and wanted so much from life. The honey that dripped from love's vessel gave way to the adventures of life's temptations. I now blush when I think of things I dropped into and allowed myself to relish. I see how easily I placed a blindfold around God's eyes so I could tenaciously play in the forbidden playgrounds of life's circus.

Rain, rain don't go away, cleanse me still for another day!

The purification came through showers of holy water. The rain bathed my soul as it gently murmured, "shame, shame go away. Come again another day."

I continued to look out my window and felt deep compassion and forgiveness for that young woman in her 30s and 40s. I saw promises brought forward by nature's spring cycle. I saw the beauty of my life and the gratitude for each of those misdemeanors – experiences that gifted me with the power of self-knowing, self-love, growth, insights, and so many blessings.

In minutes, the clouds disappeared, and the sun burst through. The warm rays embraced my vulnerable body as I wiped away my tears. I took a deep breath. My cracked, but well-healed heart began to sing again:

Shame, shame go away, come again another day.

Or not.

THE BODY KEEPS SCORE
JESSE GROS

Lying on the floor in deep lumbar pain. I texted my neighbor, "I think I need an ambulance. I need an epidural!" He hesitated, "Are you sure?" I have never been in this much pain before. My 3-year-old had just jumped on my belly in just the right/wrong place, sending waves of nauseating pain from my lower lumbar up my spine. "This must be what labor feels like," I thought.

Just as I was about to ask for the ambulance again, I heard a faint little voice say, "Just listen." It was a child's voice, soft and innocent. And yet it came from an age before words. "I'm listening," I whispered, writhing in pain. "I'm listening. I'm listening!" My voice got louder in my desperation, "I'm listening, I'm listening, I'm listening. . . ." It became a mantra – deep, exasperated words, passing, thumping with the pain, waves of nausea emanating from the depths of me. "I'm listening. . . ."

And there, suspended in my mind's eye, right in front of me like a 3-D hologram, four children's wooden letter blocks, painted in white and pastel colors. Light blue, soft yellow, pink and light green, the letters were arranged in order. They spelled out R-A-P-E. "I believe you," I said. "I believe you. I believe you. I will never forget. I will never forget." A sacred promise. "I'm listening," I pleaded. And then, in a blink, like someone turned off the main power generator on the grid, the pain stopped. The energy in the room dropped from chaos to peace. I could physically feel and see the energy in the room drop. Vroom. . . .

Then I heard a word: "Mom."
The awareness hit me like truth.
I had always known my beloved mother was the key to all of this.
She was the gatekeeper of family secrets.

This body of mine had been trying to tell me something for a long time.
With my chronic stomach and back issues, it had been trying to tell me something.
It finally brought me to my knees, so I could listen.

I'm listening, little one.
I'm listening, Mom.
I'm listening.

"MY LIPS, THESE TITS,
MY DIMPLED VOLUMINOUS HIPS
SWAYING FROM SIDE TO SIDE
HOLDING ME LIKE A CHURCH
CONGREGATION SALUTATIONS. "

— Lauryn Hill

CHAPTER 6

This Body of Mine

THIS BODY

LAURYN HILL

My lips, these tits
My dimpled voluminous hips
Swaying from side to side
Holding me like a church congregation
Salutations. I see you for who you really are
Soft and slender, or bumpy and bruised
So confused
Why do you grow so?
So disconnected,
So struck with fear
Like a lightning bolt, a jolt to the heart
That will wake you up
Sleep with me, he proposed with a ring
I put it on my middle finger to the sky
Is it the moment or the guy?
Time flies
Like tiny drops of lemon
Squeezed into a skinned knee
Oh, how it burns
Oh, how it awakens the depths of my pained soul
Or my pained body
A capsule of light, bright and airy
Like a refrigerator with food on the inside
Keeping me warm
Keeping me turned on,
Revved up, ready to go
Sex you say? No, I meant soup
The kind you eat without a spoon
But a spoon feels so good

My body pressed against yours
Behind closed doors
You decorate me with ink and metal
So I can be your masterpiece,
Your piece of ass,
Your makeup caked on, unrecognizable beauty
Your definition of divine
Forget me not,
Forgot by the back parking lot
The things we pretend not to know
It's like slow motion
Breathed into every pore
And then they call her a whore
But for what?
What she does with her body,
The body keeps the score
All these judgments and labels
Tiny fables, running rampant through our ears
I plugged mine
Not with fingers
But with rose quartz in the shape of your heart
Darling, just be here now
Be here with me as I drift off into dreamland
Where I can disconnect from my body and finally be free
Freedom doesn't come naturally
Naturally speaking
Nature dominates me mentally
And physically,
Physically I shake and shiver
Get cut and blistered
But I still show up to dance the tango
And devour the delectable mango juices
As I let them run down my cheeks and onto my bare chest
How sweet and sticky
All these feelings
So frisky,
So radioactive,

Activating every particle of dynamite
Bursting into flames
Ashes into dust,
Into stars flickering in the night sky
As we sing a lullaby
And the baby body cries
As it starts all over again

STUNTMAN
MICK BREITENSTEIN

Dear Old Friend,

Most would say that we don't look that old.
We have a pretty good facade going, but we both know better.
We know the damage we have done.
Remember when we climbed mountains, jumped over cars and off of skyscrapers?
Through fire, car crashes?
I treated you like an indestructible unit.
Youthful ignorance, I suppose.
Who would have thought we couldn't devour an entire pizza pie on our own anymore?
But we were having fun.
The time of our lives.
Bumps, bruises, concussions, broken bones. Remember that time we sat in the chiropractor's office, and he asked us to list some of our injuries and ailments?
He had to stop us and call for his assistant to come in and take notes, so they could get it all down?
I even felt a bit of pride sharing it all with him and still standing, still alive, and able to tell him all about it.
I never meant to abuse you or take you for granted.
I thought, in a way, that I was honoring you by pushing you to your limits, using you to your full potential.
Even with all of this, you've been reliable.
All things considered.
I should have gone to the dentist more, stretched more, more yoga, more breathing, a lot more.
I think maybe growing up in a household of men, I forgot the power of being soft.
I used to think, "maybe I should have taken up dance," but even in that world,

the outcome probably would have been the same.

I wish I had learned about nutrition earlier in life and not put so many processed toxins in our system.

The decades of chronic marijuana use, the hard partying through our twenties...

We certainly are feeling it now, aren't we?

I am sorry.

It's not too late for us.

Healing has begun.

Care and consideration have been restored.

There is nothing left to prove.

Nobody would care anyway.

We did have some fun, didn't we?

Diving and surfing.

Almost drowning in the rip current at Zuma Beach, even though we knew better than to be in the water that day.

I could have listened to you more.

Paid more attention.

Maybe we'd have less aching now.

Maybe we'd get out of bed a little easier in the morning.

I feel the change, as I know you do.

We walk now.

There is nowhere to get to.

No sprint, or race to win.

We could write a book about all our adventures, the risks we took, and survived.

Funny, it never felt like our true nature, did it?

But we could, so we did.

Regret is not on the table.

Here we are now, awake, alive and aware.

It is our time to slow down, be gentle, restore, and replenish.

Breathe, walk, sit quietly, peacefully.

I know, you know, I still get tempted.

I miss the rush of pushing up against another body in the heat of competition or the thrill of combat.

The rush of flying through the air, dunking the ball through the hoop, diving off a high cliff.

I accept where we are.

My responsibility in it all.

And discovering what was passed on to us, inherited; the rounded shoulders that we share with our siblings and grandfather, the quick temper and resorting to using our fists to end a disagreement.

But that's not ours.

It was passed down the lineage and we no longer have to accept ownership.

I enjoy our time now; the daily stretching and restorative work we do.

The long, slow walks in the woods.

The commitment to breathe.

Getting on the inversion board, the stationary bike.

We did our best with the knowledge we had.

I trust that together we can mend, heal, transform.

To feel free from chronic pain and feel supple again.

It's gotten easier now, knowing our limitations.

To decline invitations to engage in some of those old activities.

That silly ego that got the best of us at times.

Sometimes I think it was a form of protection.

Like a bird fluffing its colorful feathers.

Let them all witness what this body can do, the pain and abuse it can endure.

Let them imagine what it could do to them if they fucked with us.

And sure enough, it mostly worked.

No one really fucks with us.

And that scares me a bit now.

Like an aging wolf in a pack.

When they see we have softened, when we no longer feel the need to display our physical attributes, will they attack?

See our kindness as weakness and attack?

It's silly, I know, but I've relied on you for protection for so long to help me protect those I love.

I can feel a bit lost at times.

How do I operate in the world?

Aging and becoming an old man, vulnerable.

Who will chop the wood, fix the roof, shovel the snow?

Perhaps it is time to allow spirit to take over and trust her guidance.

Detach from the physical and meld into the metaphysical.

I got it from here.

You rest.

THIS BODY IN TIME

IONA RUSSELL

I see you, my beautiful, weathered friend. I see the shadow of my past in your soul. I rejected you. I hurt you. I tried to drown you out and hide you.

I tried to take the essence of life from you in my youth, but you did not die.

I tried to drown you in toxic substances;
I tried to starve you, then stuff you;
I tried to detach from you and hide.

No matter how I tried, how I hated you, loathed you, you hobbled along, with the love and resilience of my mother's love, my ancestor's wisdom, my eternal spirit fighting through, waiting for the mask to dissolve and love to burst free from behind the locked door within.

As we enter the hallway of the crone, I finally see you, love you, and know that you are my keeper, my vessel, my ethereal lover.

Thank you, I see you; I love you.
I love all of me, embodied in you.

We are together for such a short time. I promise to enjoy you, celebrate you, love you as you are, as we are – as one, fully-integrated on this earthly plane.

Here in love.

I remember as a young child the joy of running through the wild hills in pure bliss, talking to the wild things, and seeing, being, enjoying.

I remember when I chose to separate from you, hide who we were, to dissociate and dissolve, disappear and lock my heart.

I'm sorry it took decades to come home to you, to reconnect, to remember, to embody you.

Please forgive me for my lack of trust in you.

I love you completely, unconditionally.

Thank you for carrying me home all the time.

I lost trust in you. You weren't living up to my expectations. Like a battered coastline, I expected you to overcome the storms and not erode away, and I expected you to fulfil the image I had. I expected so much of you, but never gave you support, or love, or understanding.

It's taken me 50 years to reach this new chapter.

I see as I started to return home to you, 8 years ago, you saved me; you led me with curiosity to meditation, to survive. You gave me strength and support, to break free and start my true journey home to you, emotionally, physically and spiritually.

I thank you for your patience,
I see you.
I love you.
Together for this brief moment in time,
I promise to hear you, to listen
And BE with you.

THIS BODY OF MINE
ASTRID VINEYARD HERBICH

This one precious body of mine.
This living thing, vessel, vehicle, this vulnerable, vital thing.
My teacher, my challenge, my joy, my judge.

How far we've come together on this wild journey.
We've taught one another how to crawl and walk and touch and cry,
To sing, to shout and dance.
You give sound to my laughter, expression to my moods,
You turn my sorrow to tears and my worries to wrinkles,
You give release to my ecstasy and make my pain your pain.
And you remember everything.

Even things that came long before me.
The stuff you are made of has travelled generations and galaxies.
And you know this and remember.

When I sit with you and become still enough, you speak to me in the most
subtle of languages, sensations on my skin and feelings deep in my bones.
You speak of fluidity, movement and constant change.

You are not solid, cut in stone, precious body.

As I change, you change.

My every thought flows through you like ripples on a lake and you undulate
and shift, and this thought too, you will remember for me.

Yet, all my life I have judged you so harshly.
Everything I never liked about myself I have projected onto you.
I have never expected anything less than perfection from you and have hated

every flaw I ever found in you, have hated how inadequate you made me feel.

For how could I give myself permission to walk this earth and be seen unless I was perfect?

When I was four years old, I saw my first Prima Ballerina.
Her beauty and grace took my breath away, her movement mesmerized me.
Later my mother told me she couldn't get me to move out of people's way.
And that was it.
The picture of what a body should be, an expression of something magical and ethereal, never left me.

I didn't want to walk this earth, I wanted to dance and glide over it.
But you, precious body, weren't flexible enough, weren't strong enough and I didn't get into the renowned ballet school.
And oh, how disappointed I was in you.
I buried my need to dance deep inside of you and kept it locked away for half my life.

But we grew up and people would say I was beautiful, but what they meant was that they thought you were beautiful.
But I knew you weren't perfect, and they were wrong, and I was ugly, and I didn't like it when people looked at me.
Getting attention felt threatening and dangerous.
There were predators out there and I knew it.
I wanted to hide. I had to hide.

And you listened.
We gained some weight, we built some walls, the hurt still happened, but you took the brunt.
You did all that for me, and still I resented you for it, for showing me and the world just how scared I really was.

We've worked since then, you and me, dear body.

I have learned what a precious gift you are.
We've danced together, spirit and body.

You've lent yourself to me as an instrument in so many ways, have let me express through you so much of who I am, and I want you to know how grateful I am.

Grateful for your patience, your resilience, strength, wisdom and guidance.

You have healed me over and over again, in so many ways.
And I love you.

I promise you, I will do my best to keep you strong and subtle and safe, to nourish you and listen to your needs.
And most of all, I promise to protect you from my harsh thoughts and my judgment.
You deserve better than that.

We will keep changing as we get older, and I want to be able to walk that path gracefully with you,
Enjoying every step and honoring how far we've come.
Together.

"LOVING YOURSELF ISN'T VANITY, IT'S SANITY."

— Andre Gide

CHAPTER 7

Becoming Human

YOU ARE WHOLE AND COMPLETE, AND YET UNFINISHED

JESSE GROS

"You are not a troubled guest on this earth,
You are not an accident amidst other accidents
You were invited…" - David Whyte

Your illusion of future wholeness is just that, an illusion.
You will never be whole and complete.
In the future, that is.
You are whole and complete now.
Completely flawed, yes.
Like all of us.
Like a perfectly-cooked lasagna with burnt edges.

"Hey! I like those burnt edges!" you protest.
Me, too.
I love your burnt edges.
They go well with mine.

Your beauty lies in your range.
Dark.
Light.
Beautiful thoughts.
Ugly thoughts.
Beautiful actions.
Ugly actions.

Like Tyle Durdon from Fight Club says:
"You will never be complete."

Thank God.

How boring would it be to get "there" before it's over?

A titillating paradox, indeed.

Whatever shame – spoken or not.

Whatever action – taken or not taken.

All can be forgiven.

Not when you die.

Not in heaven.

But now.

Right now.

As in... this lifetime.

Whatever moral trespass has you believing that you are not worthy,

Or that you are not enough,

It's a lie.

But you don't believe me, do you?

If only you knew my darkness, you say,

You would not think me worthy of salvation.

Trust me, my friend.

I have done ugly.

I have thought ugly.

No matter how shiny on the outside.

There is always something hidden from view.

What do you keep inside for fear others would recoil?

What have you done that makes you think you are irreconcilable in the eyes
of the universe?

You are wrong.

It's a trap.

A well-crafted lie to keep you seeking salvation outside of yourself.

Fear of the light.

Fear of flight.

Your ego lives in a small town in the mountains.

On the edge of the world.
Scared of change.
Scared of the new.
A self-appointed gatekeeper.
Trading adventure for safety without your permission.

Come back to now.
You are whole... in this moment.

"You are not a troubled guest on this planet.
You were invited...."

THIS MAKES ABSOLUTELY NO SENSE AND I LOVE IT

ASTRID VINEYARD HERBICH

I think I'm done trying to make sense of life,
And make peace with the fact that God is either completely nuts,
Or just happens to have an outrageous sense of humor.

So, rather than trying to make sense of the universe
and all the things and people in it,
I think I'll just work on loving it.

All of it.
Without pulling it apart, dissecting, probing, weighing, theorizing and agonizing.

Because I don't want to look at life as a problem anymore.
A puzzle I've been given to solve.
But rather as a gift I have been given.
And my job is just to love it.

So I sit in awe, admiring it all.
The perfection of the chaos,
of all things created and deconstructed every day.
The flow of life in and out of being.

I may not have been given the brain to make sense of it all,
But I have been given the heart to love it all,
If I let it.
The beauty of it is, that I don't have to understand something
In order to love it.
I don't have to understand a person to love him or her.

I don't even have to understand myself.

I just have to hold it all, ever so gently,
For all its preciousness, in my loving heart.

You see, something surprising happens when you do that.
By simply loving something or someone unconditionally,
You actually begin to more fully understand them.

Because now you're seeing through the lens of your heart,
And the heart can see more than the mind.
You can see the essence of what is before you.
You can see the miracle and the divinity being expressed,
Right there for you, to witness.

Our hearts may not be sensible, or reasonable, or rational,
But they are wise. And hopeful beyond reason.
Never too tired to look for something to love.
Our hearts aren't happy unless they are loving.

Where the mind creates obstacles,
The heart just jumps the hurdle and fearlessly runs toward another heart.

Even after falling, breaking,
Crying and aching,
After deciding to close off,
Build walls and towers and fortresses,
Your heart will never stop longing to love.

So let it.

It may not make sense,
But you have to let it.

Just let it love.

When you do, chances are,
Even your past with all its sorrow and pain,

Will start making sense again.

Love will put it into perspective for you.
Your heart will show you the big picture,
How everything and everyone you've ever lost or longed for
Has taught you how to love and live better.

How they have made you who you are today.

How it was all for you.

And how it was all an act of love.

DANCING TOGETHER IN EARTH SCHOOL
JANELLE NELSON

Earth school has been really hard for me lately. Maybe the teacher is testing me to see if I'm ready to enter the next grade. If that's the case, I'll do my best to rise to the occasion. I don't want to have to repeat this curriculum again.

I'll be honest that my kindergarten self wants to push another student off the monkey bars today. Maybe throw my peanut butter and jelly sandwich at her, too. Doing that will guarantee I'll get assigned to kindergarten purgatory by all the heavenly teachers watching. Ok. I won't actually do it, but I'm definitely gonna picture it in my head. And I'm for sure going to stick my tongue out at her while no one's looking.

I'm reminding myself earth school comes in waves. Sometimes it's stormy, and in other seasons can be picturesque like summer break. Summer break will come again. It will.

But for now, what is my lesson? My lesson is to grow up the part of myself that is passive and meek. The aspect of me that goes into paralyzing fear at the thought of having to growl at someone. Am I still kind? Am I still loving? Did the best parts of me die as I started to growl? No, they are still there. They are still there, right? I can't feel those parts of me when I growl.

Maybe the secret sauce is to be direct and precise like an ice pick. Not mean, not aggressive, but mathematically assertive. *My nervous system just settled as I wrote that.* Clear, direct and to the point, that's my medicine. I want my adult self to teach my kindergartener to not throw her peanut butter and jelly sandwich when she needs to speak her mind. Instead, showing her to speak with calm, grounded authority. I want my adult self to show up for my inner teenager, who was picked on and never spoke her mind. We are done with that.

Growing pains – real growing pains – stretching me into a place of deep discomfort. I want to cry, throw up, and sometimes jump with excitement all at the same time. I once read that grief is a portal of transformation. I have been grieving the death of a past version of myself and it's all a bit disorienting. The adult part of me knows I must metabolize my grief to move forward. Otherwise I'll stay stuck in kindergarten, 2nd grade, 7th grade or 10th grade purgatory.

I love 10th grade Janelle. She's a sweetheart and is known by her friends and family as a safe, empathetic person. I look back at her now and I see her differently. I know about her future, living with an autoimmune disease. I know it comes from the stress of not speaking her truth. I want her to have a backbone. I want her to find her anger and her voice. I love her, but I want more for her. She's not going to be liked by everyone now, and that's ok. Some part of her has to die. And it's ok, because she deserves that updated version of self-respect.

Do no harm. Take no shit. Thanks for the lesson, earth school. Can I graduate now?

BECOMING HUMAN
PATRICK FAULWETTER

Sean Penn's character in *Tree of Life* says: "One day we break down and cry and understand it all – all things." That quote always touched me deeply, probably because my subconscious knew I was far from experiencing it. Maybe it is not one moment but several. For me, these moments of breaking down in awe of the universe are rare.

It took me twenty-seven years for the first of these moments to occur, touching and being touched by the spirit of the lands of the American Southwest. The second was standing in the center of the endless grasslands of the Dakotas, feeling the warm wind stroke my back as a supercell approached.

The third time was sitting in a sacred circle chanting with the shaman during a beautiful night-time ceremony. In-between these moments were long stretches of earning certificates, navigating, accumulating, and building my identity. In these stretches of time, I often felt happiness, but had a hard time acknowledging my deeper humanity.

My inner world, where I felt safe and felt joy, was split off from the outside world. On the outside, the battle for survival was fought amongst the giant machines of reason and logic. Other people seemed to be okay in that war-ravaged world; they could even find and make sense of love out there, but I couldn't find it.

I never experimented with drugs. I had my first girlfriend in my twenties. Why would I engage in all those outer distractions, which kept me from my cherished inner lands? I grew up with reason and logic in a society traumatized by its own atrocities committed during the second World War. A trauma my culture tried to mend through the mind, through reason and logic. I always felt that our mind-centric, rigid approach to life led the Germans to do the unspeakable in the first place. And there we were, using the same way of relating to the world, hoping for a different result.

I needed to escape the fear and collective guilt, so I left my country and moved to California, where my nervous system could rest. When I arrived that first evening, I could feel something was right. I had made the right choice. And I could start the journey to self-expression and healing that my soul had longed for all these years.

REALLY BAD IDEAS
ASTRID VINEYARD HERBICH

The worst thing about really bad ideas is that they seem brilliant at the time. Your ego latches onto them, swallows them whole and runs with them, no matter who tries to stop us or tackle us to the ground to save us from our own insanity.

No, we keep running and the longer we run, the more energy and time we've put into it, the faster we run, trying to convince ourselves and others that indeed this is a great idea.

But here's the thing: No matter how fast we run, we know.
Some part of us always knows.
Always tries to steer us right, tries to make us see the truth and tell the ego to cease and desist.

But Really Bad Ideas will not go quietly into the night, no, they will put up a fight.
They will find the best arguments, sound as logical as the day is long, or turn away and stick fingers into their ears and go "La-La-La-La" until that voice quietly gives up for a while.

That voice telling you:
"Yes, this man is insanely attractive, he makes your heart skip a beat just by the way he looks at you so tenderly and longingly.
But he is also unavailable. So, don't go there."
Yes, you should listen to that voice.
And no, of course I didn't.

The voice telling you:
Don't go to this stupid audition.
You'll get the part, you'll feel good about getting it and do it just to boost your

ego and you will regret it later because it will be a giant waste of your time."
You should listen to that voice.
And no, of course I didn't.

The voice telling your hormone-riddled body:
"You don't need to eat that entire chocolate bar, you've already devoured two muffins and a half jar of applesauce, you're good."

"Yes, but the muffins were vegan and gluten-free, so that doesn't count and the applesauce unsweetened, I just added a little bit of maple syrup, so really, none of that counts!"

Well, I usually listen to that second voice. It's very convincing. And chocolate-flavored.

We all have bad ideas.
Some are worse than others and some are very good at pretending to be quite innocent and inconsequential.

Texting while driving. I have to constantly remind myself:
You could actually kill someone doing this. And you would never get to take it back.
You can never go back to this moment and say:
"No, I can send this smiley emoji when I've parked."

You never get to take back that unkind word you said to a stranger, just because you were having a bad morning.
Or that thoughtless joke you made, that she took the wrong way and hurt her.

The biggest and smallest decisions we make ripple out into this world, and they affect and change us and everything around us.

And often we don't know which decisions are big, which ones are small. We don't know what kind of wave we create in the fabric and frequency of Everything That Is.

One word. One smile. One text. One touch. One deep breath.

We make big and small decisions every day and the only guide to steer us right is our heart.

When you said that word, how did that make your heart feel?

When you smiled at that lonely-looking stranger, did the place in the center of your chest contract or open?

When you gave that loving touch, what kind of ripple did that send through your body and from there out into the world?

We have a guidance system. A heart GPS.
But we have to install it and cultivate it.
And we have to listen.

We have to learn to discern what feels good and what feels right.
Our egos want to be fed, want to feel good and bold and strong.
But our soul wants to feel good for everyone.

If this choice of mine is only good for myself and serves only my own immediate needs, but may hurt someone else down the line, my soul knows.
And it will close my heart.
Constrict my breath.
Clench my jaw.

Our soul knows that we suffer with and for each other.
We feel each other's pain and joy, for we are here together.

Sending waves of kindness, harshness, lovingness, healing, hurting, compassion, or forgiveness onto each other's shores.

Feel the waves.
Watch out for the bad ideas.
Try to listen to the voice in your heart.
It will always steer you right.

SPARK

ANJ BEE

It started with just a spark –
The glass shattered on the wooden panels of the past,
Etched with each memory – an imprint of what was.
A crystal ball containing each fantastical illusion of what could've been,
And my higher self dropped it from the rafters above,
Deafened by the roar of memories and aspirations exploding from its sphere.

I swung down from the rafters,
Sifting through each shard,
Hunting for the remains of what I was.
A loyal friend.
A traitor.
A redemption-seeking villain.
A hopeless romantic.
A terrified misanthrope.
A thieving pirate.
A generous soul.
A miserly scoundrel.
An egomaniac.
A forlorn child.
A free-spirited tumbleweed.
A merciless shark.
An intuitive empath.
A cultural apostate.
Or perhaps I was all of these things. The whole me, held in a tight spherical
glass. Each fragment of me growing larger. The sum of the parts unable to be
contained,
Intensifying pressure upon that inner sphere,
Until the excruciating pain of the shards began sticking through my rib cage,

And my higher-self decided it was time and led me up to the rafters for an unexpected show.

Self-inquisition.
That is what some call it.
The process of exploring each stone – turned or unturned,
Was I right or wrong? Am I good or bad? Did I do right or wrong? Did I do enough in the end? Was I being fair, or treated fairly in return? Should my actions or heart be judged? Should I judge the heart or actions of others? Do I have the strength to guide us through it? Should anyone in such a heightened state of self-inquisition be running a company? Does any of it matter?

For what truly matters in the end?
And at that question, I stopped sifting through the shards of what was.
In the silence after the din, grace in the stillness,
A soft lyrical melody floating on the breeze,
Carrying wisps of hope and clarity.

The "I" after the glass shattered
It is still stepping gingerly through life,
Afraid of being seen,
Longing to blast into another outer dimension experience,
Where it feels the most expansive and free.
Maybe in this next decade, I will find my grounding in mother earth.
Find my soul and serenity on this planet,
Instead of the outer sphere.

Self-inquisition.
Is it worthwhile?
A superpower?
Or an Achilles heel?
The scalpel with which I dissect my mind as I try to understand this new "I."
A sapling attempting to grow in a tempestuous windstorm,
And as I attempt to barricade this new "I" from the shards of my former self, from the blade I frantically apply to my mind, and the torrential bullets of self-judgment,
Perhaps it's time.

Time to stop sifting through the glass,
Time to stop shooting bullets at that poor sapling swaying in the windstorm,
And do the only thing that truly matters in the end…
To love, to spin in a tutu, and to chill the fuck out, and eat some chicken tikka.

WHEN INSPIRATION STRIKES
IONA RUSSELL

When inspiration strikes, I'm mostly naked – well, completely naked, in fact, and cleansing my soul, from top to toe, tip to tap, fizzling, frothing and foaming, surrendering to the moment with eyes... gently... closed.

Rinsing the soapsuds, remembering, recognizing, repeating, releasing, freewheeling, feeling free, free as a bird... an open channel to the inspiration – wherever it may strike.

And BOOM, there it is!

Tip and a tap splitter spatter splat.

BOOM there it is... shhhhhh....

As yesterday's dirt dances down the plughole, an old ideology purified-petrified-placated and washed away – a new OPULENT scrummy interesting, delicious-stimulating-curious-cosmic idea with the tipping and the tapping. Drops. Into. My. Heart. PLOP!

I know I'm not the only one who feels the cosmic calling, colliding and knocking on the door with creative, juicy ideas ready to ignite and inspire, even if you're feeling a little insecure.

Hmmmm – Why am I naked... again... Oh well....

I was told that the reason we – I'm including you in this, so pardon the preloaded presumptions and the bare-naked souls. The rather resonating reason – being – is that the tip and the tapping and the splitter and the spattering splat of water drops, meeting our heads, is because it is God's frequency – knock – knock – knocking trying to get into our heads, with 7.8Hz, also known as the Schuman resonance.

I've no idea if this is true – does it really matter? When divine inspiration strikes, we must seize the day. Even if we are naked, or perhaps even more so, doing it naked. Hey, let's all get naked!

Hmmmmm. . . .

Do you hear the whispers, the murmurs, amusing and amassing, gathering up the crescendo with laughing limericks to taunt and tease, waiting to pull the rug or towel out from under or over us? It's the tea party of gremlins, patiently, but not so quietly, waiting for us down the hall.

What shall we do with them?

There's an empty seat waiting for us to join them. Shall we sit?

Ah – There's Mrs. Doubt. She sure is a firecracker, conquering continents of epic self-doubt. You think it's a coup, but she's just here to undermine you, and shatter your resolve. . . .

And to her right is the stern Mr. Fascist with his spreadsheets billowing out of his laptop, of every misdemeanor mistake, and failed mission. Ooooh, every failed mission. Ouch… that's gotta hurt. He's a bit of a party pooper, isn't he?

And Madame Snake, slithering in, pretending to be on our side. But she continues to subtly compare us to all those others.

Have you seen the OTHERS?!?
Who are all doing so much better than us? Ah, who are we to complain, for we should not compare. She does it with such sublime grace that you honestly believe she has your best interests at heart. But between you and me, she's a bit of a dark heartless horse, and would be better, suitably discussed as a wolf perhaps, in sheep's clothing if you get my drift. . . .

Breathe deeply, my love, and let them have their fun. One can't beat a bully at their own game. They're already ahead and they cheat, anyway. They hide cards up their sleeves like a hoodlum's game of gangster's paradise, of chance and casino Russian roulette.

Come, let's cut them a slice of this beautiful cake, baked with sugars of love, heaps of inspiration and downloads of divination, risk-takers spice, visionary nutmeg, sprinkles of free-wheeling-gypsy-hearted dancing, buckets of Magic and Mandy! It's so delicious – like a gigantic hug from the heights of the Ecstatic. Effervescent. . . SSSsspace. . . .

A love-filled embrace. . . .

We'll poison them with our potion and invite them to dance, killing them with kindness and death by compliments.

Turn the music up, DJ, let's all get naked and dance in the shower.

YOU MUST DO YOUR ART

JESSE GROS

You must do your art.
It's a fact.

You must breathe.
Also, a fact.

For many of us, art is breathing.
It's breath for the soul.

Society needs art.
The world needs art.

All children are artists.
Many of them lose it.
Or society strips it away.

Artistic expression is the breath of humanity.
It moves energy and transmutes it from contained to expressed.

Unused creative energy can become toxic.
It turns into toxic thoughts, feelings, and actions.

Red paint.
Blue chalk.
Yellow glitter.

Get some mama.

Words on the page.
Release those pent-up emotions into the world.

To entertain.
To enlighten.
To lift up.
To inspire.
To make others laugh.
To make you laugh.
To release others from their pain.
To release you from your pain.

We MUST do our art.
You MUST do your art.

The world needs more art.
That's for sure.
And guess what? So do you.
Get some.
Share some.

Paint naked with your lover,
While eating dim sum.
Now, that sounds fun.

An email from a friend:
"I decided not to die... fuck it, I'll make art."
She has pulled herself away from the cliff many times with art.
I get it.

I lost my art.
But it found me.
It came back.

Like soul food.
Like a lost love.
It came back.

"YOU TRY TO DROWN YOUR
SORROWS... SHOULDN'T HAVE
TAUGHT THEM HOW TO SWIM!"

— John Craigie

CHAPTER 8

Hope

HALLELUJAH!
ASTRID VINEYARD HERBICH

Hallelujah, world.
Hallelujah, love.
Hallelujah, pain.
Hallelujah to everything we've lost and everything we've gained.
Hallelujah to every hurt we have inflicted upon each other.
Hallelujah to your healing touch.
Hallelujah to everything we've taken from this world.
Hallelujah to the gifts each and every life has brought.
Hallelujah to the sacred.
Hallelujah to the darkness.
Blessed be the tears I've shed and all the ones I have denied.
Blessed be the laughter, the sound of a soul awakening.
Blessed be all women and men, my sisters and brothers,
stumbling through this life
Bumping into and away from each other,
Trying to figure things out, themselves and each other and life.
All of us blind until our hearts can see.

May we be blessed by a God who gives a damn,
And a Goddess who doesn't know damnation.

May we all be blessed by whichever part of us remembers what it means to
be divine,
Sacred unto itself.
Life giving of itself so everything can live.
The only true love the one that lives deep inside of us,
Unconditionally loving it all,
Singing Hallelujah to the dawn and the dew
And the demolition crew.

Hallelujah to letting things go
Letting things change
And going with the flow.

Hallelujah to times of rest and stillness and to being bored.
Hallelujah to this breath.
Hallelujah to pen and paper, paintbrushes and pianos.
Hallelujah to the beauty all around us.
Hallelujah to the vastness of the cosmos
And all the tiny things I can hold in the palm of my hand.

I pray for the small things and the vast empty space.
I pray for peace in our hearts.
I pray you are happy.
I pray I can bring happiness to this world.
I pray for all beings, visible and invisible.
May you be happy and healthy,
Peaceful and wealthy in all the ways that matter most.
May you know love, my love.
May you be seen and heard and touched and witnessed in all your beauty.
May you never forget:
You are a Hallelujah.

HOPE DEALER / DOPE HEALER

JESSE GROS

Hope dealer.
Sharing hope of the brightest kind.
Close encounters of the heart-opening kind.
Is there nothing more hopeful than love?
Is there nothing more captivating than new love?
Or even just interest?
The possibility of love. . . .

Without love, there is nothing.
A dry, barren desert.
Lots of trying.
Lots of story.
Life on-hold.
Held in stasis.

Like an African frog frozen in time under the mud of a dry lake,
Waiting for its chance to spring into life when the waters return.
Our hearts frozen in stasis.
Waiting for the waters of hope and love and lust to return.
So that we may hop around in joy once more.

The hope dealer didn't promise happily ever after.
She just said that it – could be.
And that, my dear, is enough to sustain most for a very long time.
What could be – it's shinier than what is – almost always.
Because it's painted in the clouds out of glitter and gold.
It's free of the messiness of humanity.

Churches are built on it.
The entire space program is built on it.

What *could* be.
What if?

It's enough for me.
Sign me up.
Send me a link to your GoFundMe page.
I'll pay for a shot glass worth of jet fuel.
So many of us are hope dealers for each other.
We need it.
We breathe into what is possible,
Through the lived experience of those around us.

To live without hope.
Now that is unbearable.

But what would the Buddhists say?
Would they say the hope dealer is bad?
Would they say that hope lives in the future?
Hope takes you out of the present?
I'm not sure.
And I'm just fine with it.

Hope dealer, hook me up with another dime bag, please.
I hear California has completely legalized hope.
Pretty much anyone can get some.
You don't have to know someone to get some anymore.
Hell, you can have it delivered to your house!
Hope on-tap.
Now that's innovation.

THERE IS NOTHING WRONG WITH YOU

IONA RUSSELL

Are you sure? I've pondered this and wondered this, agonized and radicalized, waited out the musings, bewildered and bamboozled, dancing around in circles like a one-eyed peg-legged pirate.

And do you know what? I never did conclude one way or the other. But there is one thing I am certain of: it's that I did indeed choose this cosmic merry-go-round path, this unfolding and unravelling magical existence!

Would you like some puzzle tea with your curious cream cake? Don't worry, we are all quite mad around here.

Let's unpack this transcendental leather-bound treasure box and see what we can find. . . .

Did you know that the Buddhist's believe – well, according to my dear deceased stepdad – that children choose their parents, the daughters choose the father, and the sons choose the mother. I was not impressed by this mess I'd chosen: a father so rigid, dishonest, unforgiving, harsh and judgemental, shaming and blaming and yet taking no responsibility for his orchestrated deeds, putting them on the self-righteous shelf – "Do as I say, not as I did!"

Well, let me tell you – that did not vibe with me, and I skedaddled and paddled up the river of self-loathing, without a paddle – it did not flow well in those wondering, wonder years.

Yet there were moments of sweetness. A few, I remember, wrapped in candy cane, a little too sweet, as he suited and booted up to leave Santa footprints to entertain our wild, youthful and unstoppable imaginings on Christmas mornings.

Why did I choose this man? Did I choose him as a father?

Did you choose yours? It's a bit of a bitter pill to swallow.

Here, have some more puzzle tea.

Hmmm, where were we?

Ah, yes.

In a vision, gazing thru the mists of deep healing, I saw myself choosing this life, seeing my pain, seeing my misbegotten, traumatic birth, nearly dying before I began (that would have been a very short chapter). I literally saw a kaleidoscopic mirage of all my lives, and all possibilities and all that would unfold, could unfold, with all the infinite variables – like an ayahuasca vision board, floating in front of me – all for my choosing, and this is what I chose. (There were no drugs involved this time.)

Hey, would you like some sugar in your puzzle tea?

You might be wondering where the gentle nurturing and my heart were held.

It was my mother, who wrapped us in safety and security like warm velvet marshmallow Hershey™ kisses, washed down with a heaping of hugs, and sprinkles of helium balloons filled with unconditional love. No matter what I did – and let me tell you, I certainly tried – to burst those big, m-fing balloons. But they were un-burstable!

So now what – where does this leave our discussion? Eh, who knows, none of us gets out of here alive, that's for sure. Let's roll the dice and have another slice of mystic pizza pie.

There is nothing wrong with you or me, except for what we choose to put in our human picnic basket. We gather, collect, adopt, carry, witness, take on the patterns and illusions of the masquerade ball around us, hiding behind Venetian masks of identity, along with the boxes we squeeze into and keep on the shelf.

The journey is to unpack that ridiculously-rambunctious-heavy-burdensome-outdated-tacky basket, to lay it down, tip it out and cleanse in the pool.

Shedding the illusions and rebirth anew, let it all go and live here now, in this moment, and put down that puzzle tea. There is nothing wrong with you or me. We are all quite mad.

BEYOND THE MACHINE, THERE WAS LIFE
JESSE GROS

Out beyond the grinding metal and whirling wheels there was life.

Out beyond the rigid frames, oppressive structures and suffocating rules, there was life.

Fear had taken hold of everything inside the machine.
Metal on metal.

Fear, rigidity, oppression and competition. These were the great pillars that supported infinite growth at all costs. All powers leaned towards the greatest value of all: efficiency. Efficiency at all costs! Efficiency at all angles and all perspectives, squeezing the juice from the sacred into little vials to be added to the latest new lipstick. This one is "spiritual lipstick." It has real shaman blood in it. Wear it, and you, too, will be one with the universe. What's that? How much does it cost? Well, you will have to talk to our loan department first.

The machine spun its web and made everything into its own image. Education, created to mirror the factory. Healthcare designed to honor the machine. We kill you to make you better. Mass produced, mass seduced into a kind of low-level, never-ending illness. Stress is normal. Poor sleep is normal. Obesity is normal. All-can-be-cured with a pill. Step in line please, you will get your turn.

Food, entertainment, clothing, living – all fashioned after the assembly line. Each thing we used to do for each other gobbled up and resold, commodified. Churn, churn, crank, crank. . . bellowing smoke.

And the machine fed itself on souls. Trade your soul for safety. Trade your soul for healthcare. Trade your future for a new pair of shoes. I'll have the gold-plated Jordans, please.

And when the machine broke down, like addicts, we addressed the failure by doing even more of the same, hoping that this time some miracle would happen. The soil is failing; it needs even more fertilizer. The people are depressed; they need a new, new, new drug. The animals are not producing; they, too, need a new, new, new drug.

And there were those who tried to stop the world eating machine. They tried to convince those in power; it was too hungry. "We hear you," they said. We hear your grievances, but we can't just turn it off! The people would go hungry. The depressed would go unmedicated. The children would stop learning! *How will they compete?* How will they win? Even though they are losing. . . .

And this argument went on for decades. Nothing ever changed.

But outside the boundaries, outside the steel walls of the world eating machine, there were wild places. Places the machine had barely touched. Living on those islands of thought, in those green pastures of possibility, people spoke of the machine as if it was "out there." They knew it was off in the distance, even though they could not see it.

And beyond the machine, there was life – people who took responsibility for their own health and education. People who treated the children like precious beings instead of investments in their future. People who understood that we are not widgets, we are not consumers; we are not human capital, but soft, creative protean beings. Individuals who desire to have fun, to enjoy our craft instead of laboring, with our heads down for decades, until they finally set us out to pasture.
These wild folks were not possessed by the lies of the culture.
They were not consumed by the fear.

And these folks that lived out on the edges. . . they thrived.
And they lived.
And over the years, they became the healers.
They become the leaders.

The people who escaped the machine found them.
They arrived beleaguered and wary, exhausted by their culture.

And over time, they healed.

They became who they were meant to be.

They became whole once more.

I'VE BEEN HAVING DREAMS (PART 1)

SARA FALUGO

I've been having dreams
of the underworld
of the over-culture
of the middle earth

I've been having dreams
of the last link
the last breath
a short death
and of prison cells

Ramana Maharshi
Francis Ford Coppola
spirit father
godfather
how do you fit together
in this tiny little lunchbox called human life

mine is a short tale
a long tale
a story with no beginning
and many potential endings
the ledge that I now must walk out upon
requires little of this self
there is nothing left to do
but let the batteries run out
pull the string
watch the fuzzy bunny spin in circles
until

it stops
the grand pause

shoot this arrow directly into the bull's eye
crow to my left
owl to my right
I dream of the great mystery
it is nearly time to take flight
the words all but crumble
upon falling from my lips
revealing their futility
the truth is silent

still
within
this boat
this ego
has sailed itself onto the rocky shores of the dharma
a gaping wound has left her engine flooded
drop me a line now
with a heavy sinker
it's time to go low
and deep
my whale is hiding out
in uncharted territories
collective unconscious
synchronicity

I Ching
you are everything
and nothing
just like me
all I can see is our connectedness
in truth though
connection is trite
compared to what I see
one
full stop

one
and yet the plot is just beginning to thicken
and there is so much to hold on to now
rescuers from down under
The Hero's Journey
Rabia and her many Pillagers
all of them taking
greedily consuming
the sacred chalice
just as man's greed has desecrated this earth

divine mother has started a fire
and Pachamama has finally put her foot down
will we awaken from these dreams we have been dreaming
or shall we fall more deeply into the abyss
and
does it ultimately matter

in the silence
I see
I know
that nothing ever happened
they say that when a Buddha is birthed
all of existence awakens with her
there is no more suffering
when the eyes of the beholder
dissolve beyond it
transcend the excrement
and put to rest the battle within

we are infinite
yes
and these bodies are temporary gifts
that will eventually return to dust
this drop of consciousness
will return to the ocean
and none will be the wiser

I'VE BEEN HAVING DREAMS (PART 2)

SARA FALUGO

I've been having dreams
and you know that I have
and you've been having dreams
we know that this is true as well
the question
we are left with
as we are tossed about
by this viral storm
is where exactly
will our dreams meet
how lucidly do we care to be together

would you like to dream
a new dream
with me
or shall we continue to turn
on the suffering wheel
shall we all clothe ourselves
with compassion
and call it a night
or do we prefer to remain ignorant
wandering through this house of mirrors

no judgement my friend
no judgement
my friend
perhaps this is all I need to do now
I am putting the gavel down

taking off the fancy wig and the power robe
I am moving to a land without borders
without courthouses
without churches
without abusive governments
without a military industrial complex

I am moving to a land
where it is encouraged to kiss the earth
where we roll around in the dirt and make love
where we honor the seasons
the elements
life
where we acknowledge and honor
each living being's place
in the web of life
and receive blessings
from the mother
I am moving to a land
where hierarchy is just something read about in books
and homelessness is understood
as the crown jewel of the dark ages of every-man-for-himself-ism

I am moving to a land
in my heart
where no child
young or grown
is left hungry
where everyone has a place in society
where the society is built on love
understanding
joyfulness
and generosity

I've been having dreams, yes
and for too long
they have been just dreams

you've been having dreams as well
how about we get lucid together
there was once an underground railroad
I think we may need to build one again

it is no wonder we cannot digest our food
IBS
gluten
dairy
and nearly everything else intolerant
we have been swallowing our own bullshit for too long
and shoving it down each other's throats
as the norm
intestines require harmony
and harmony does not allow another human to sleep on the streets
hungry
cold
wet from the rain
dirty
disparaged
forgotten
invisible

I've been having dreams alright
and I know that you have as well
will you take my hand now
can we walk together
have you seen enough suffering yet
shall we tear down the colosseum walls
constructed so firmly within our fearful psyches
we throw our own babies to the lions
mothers
fathers
daughters
sons
to the lions of the streets
in our concrete psycho-spiritual jungles

I've been having dreams, yes
of a new land
a new earth
a rebirth
and I have been praying for the courage
the wisdom
the guidance
to see them into reality

THESE WINGS OF MINE
ASTRID VINEYARD HERBICH

These dreams of mine,
They've taken me out and beyond.

This heart of mine has loved you throughout time.

These eyes of mine have seen your beauty everywhere.

This body of mine has danced me through the storms of life.

My arms have reached for the stars.

My tongue has tasted eternity.
It was bitter and it was sweet.

Sitting in the desert I have breathed and despaired
And came back to life.
I have lost my way in the fog again and again,
Only to remember to listen to the sound of my heart beating in my chest
And follow it home.

I have sat with my loves and looked into their eyes
And thanked them for breaking my heart.

For breaking through its rigidity,
Shattering the glass tower,
And letting me bleed.

I have felt my heart drain until empty,
Only to fill up with life again.

That's the rhythm of each life's song.
The beating of the heart,
As it opens and closes, again and again.
Never afraid to let go of the old and let in the new.
Never afraid of the next beat.
Never attached to this one drop of blood.

It keeps the red river of my life flowing
And I am grateful.

I am full.

Full of life.
Full of love.
Full of loss and laughter.
Full of tears I probably should have shed.
Maybe I will.

Or maybe they have become part of my blood,
A river of its own flowing toward the ocean of all unshed tears
Somewhere amongst the stars.

I imagine it like the Dead Sea.
On entering it holds and suspends you
And heals you.

These wings of mine can take me there and anywhere.

They are a precious gift in a time where we all hang suspended,
Sitting in our shelters, listening to the wind ravaging our world,
And waiting for the storm to pass.

Because even if my wings can't brave the outside world right now,
They can take me into the infinite space within.
Let me explore the landscape of my soul,
Let me dance to the rhythm of my heart,

And if nothing else, I can hug my inner child,

Sing her a song
And tell her it will all be okay.

And I will show her her wings and teach her how to fly.

This storm will pass by, as all storms do,
And I will have gotten used to its voice.
I might even find I'll miss its lunatic howl once it's gone.
Because it spoke to the crazy in me
And gave voice to my rage.
The part of me that wants to tear down houses
And rip out trees and throw them at mountains,
Just to make people wake up and stop taking everything so for granted.

The part of me, wise enough to be grateful
for being shaken, rattled and stirred up,
So, I'll remember that I am alive
And need to live
And need to love
And need to break
And heal
And scream and sing
And teach and learn
And create
And let go

And spread my wings

And let the wind take me away.

"BUT WE WERE WISE. WE KNEW THAT MAN'S HEART, AWAY FROM NATURE, BECOMES HARD."

- Chief Luther Standing Bear

CHAPTER 9

Mother Earth

IN THE FOREST
MARTHA JEFFERS

Deep in the forest, there was a secret, and it was time for it to be discovered.
As I lay on the ground of our sacred mountain, I silently asked the gods and goddesses who keep watch over all, how I would begin to unravel the reel of emotions that swept over me. Feeling held by the Great Mother, I began.

There was a time of great silence. A time when waters churned and winds blew clouds from the skies. I remember ever so vividly standing on the wind-blown beach watching the waves of the storming ocean hit the sands. Standing with feet firmly planted while invoking the god of my ancestors, I heard a guttural sound escape my lips. No vowels or consonants came forward. The sound made no sense. It yielded nothing. It pleaded for nothing but prayed for the fallen, the sacred, the lost, and the slaughtered.

The sounds were not of me, nor known to me, but I felt them. I stood in the presence of something holy and beyond my grasp. I released centuries of repression and the guttural sound morphed into a primal cry sent as a prayer to the God of the Universe. The roar silenced the wind and quieted the churning waters.

"How long must we hold the pain of those who have passed?" it seemed to say. How long must we walk our path, riddled with promises never met and injustices silenced away? "How long?" I asked, "how long?"

I gently brought myself back and remembered why I had entered the forest. Deep in prayer, I spoke to my mother.

How long must I contain your wounds and regrets, Madre? How long must I hold your unfulfilled life and shame? How long must I endure your unresolved rejections and self-abandonment? How long, Mother, must I contain your suffering?

The sound of great compassion often overtakes me. The canticle song I sing is reparation for all our souls, but mostly, Mother!

Deep in the forest, there was a secret, and I found you, Madre, a soul with such depth and knowing nothing could contain you until you crossed the veil, into the purity of your heart and into the arms of that perfect love.

THE VOICE OF THE EARTH
ASTRID VINEYARD HERBICH

The trees had kept it safe for longer than even they could remember.
In a place where birds would take their young on their very first flight.
Elephants would go there to die, to lay their souls down at its feet.
Lions went there to mate and play with their cubs.
Insects told soft, whispered stories about the place of life and death,
The place of in-between, where it was always dusk, or maybe dawn,
home to a thousand fireflies, always keeping guard.

Nobody knows how the forest knew it was time.
Time to let it go.
But everybody knows where they were when they first heard it.

The whisper on the wind,
The grumbling of the ground,
The song, the sigh, subtle and yet undeniable.

At first people thought they were going mad, then they assumed it must be a
strange virus afflicting the brain and causing mass delusions.

Nobody was immune, they all heard it.

The voice of the earth.

Speaking every language, knowing everything humans knew.
She had listened for so long, watched for thousands of years.
Watched and waited and hoped and given and given and given of herself.

Until the day came she asked the forest to set her voice free.
Unable to watch any longer, she needed to be heard.
And she gave them no choice.

She started with a whisper and then got louder and louder until she roared.

Some people went mad. Jumping off bridges and cliffs or walking into the wild ocean, and there was nothing anyone could do to help them.
They just couldn't stand her pain.
A lot of people just cried and cried.
But everyone stopped their lives and listened. Because they had to.
She was too loud to ignore.

And eventually they understood.
Deep in their bones, they began to understand.

That she was tired.
Tired of bleeding.
Tired of hurting.
Tired of excuses and apologies and half-hearted remedies.
She was done with empty promises, fantastical lies and wishful thinking.

So, she told them what she needed them to do.

She opened their eyes to all the damage they had done.
And then she showed them how to fix it.

When they protested and became sulky, she sent waves, wind and wildfires to wake them up and soon they knew not to resist.

They went to work.
Day and night they worked to clean up their messes.
They put all their resources, energy, money, science, invention and manpower into replanting, rebuilding, repopulating and regenerating all that had been lost.

On and on they worked, for a generation or two,
Her voice slowly but surely going from shouting to speaking and back to whispering,
Softer and softer...
Until one day,
it was gone.

And humans all around the world stopped and looked about,
Noticing that all the wars had stopped,
All the division between them had disappeared,
Poverty had turned into a cautionary tale,
Races, religion, righteousness, nothing mattered anymore.

They had all worked together towards one goal.
And they had succeeded.

And they knew she had saved them from themselves.

And they lived happily…

…for…

Well, we'll see.

THE GARDENER
ARMINDA LINDSAY

The potatoes need to be dug up. The long-dead green bean vines need to be pulled out and composted. The cucumbers haven't been harvested in at least two weeks; their ability to materialize and then immediately engorge themselves on the vine is nothing short of magical. Sadly, the cukes we have eaten, no matter how small I pick them, are bitter and no amount of salt has been their salvation. And the tomatoes — we planted 14 of them, maybe six varieties, but 14 different plants. They're prolific, to say the least. The squirrels and birds are getting well-fed on the abundant crop. I can't eat them all. We talked about salsa, tomato soup or even spaghetti sauce, but haven't picked more than three tomatoes since that wishful conversation three weeks ago.

The ground is every bit as red as the heavy-laden plants, littered after the crowd dispersed and left their fruit behind to decay without attention because the gardener is gone. He's not coming back to clean up the messiness of what he so meticulously planned and we then planted. His spreadsheets, order forms, lists, and labeled popsicle sticks now lie in piles I can't find or make order out of the weeds in their wake.

The zinnias clambering all summer long for the front seat screaming, "SHOTGUN!" are now elbowing each other in the face and tumbling toward the ground, unable to stop the stampede they started and my attempts to fence them in again look paltry in comparison to the original vision of ordered tall down the middle, medium next, then shortest on the outside, cascading heights along both lengths of the flowerbed. Is this overgrowth and death and abundance just because it's late August or is it because the master planner, the gardener, is gone? I know he's not coming back.

I love being in the garden, although double-edged for me. I feel closest to him there, weeding, transplanting, harvesting. And saddest for the same reasons.

I dug up all the potatoes. I started with the pitchfork but couldn't dig without stabbing one spud on every plunge. The potatoes were too close to the surface; they were planted just before I got here. Helpers from elsewhere came to assist; to be directed and taught by the gardener: how to turn your soil, how to lay the yardstick to measure your stakes' distance from each other, how to slip the string over the end of the opposite stake making the line taut, how to hoe down the row as you go and exactly what amount of space to leave between each hill, and how to bury them so completely to ensure their growth into brand new potatoes.

Their greens were beautiful; the prettiest the gardener had ever seen. When he went away I kept watch, kept watering, kept talking to the buried spuds. There were potatoes popping above-ground! It was too soon. They were green like their tops — I had to bury them again, had to coax them back down, give them more time, do the work that the gardener trusted others to do but they weren't deep enough. I could see evidence. Bucket after bucket after bucket of mulch I shoveled, hauled, dumped and spread. I laid a fresh and false blanket on top of the bed, urging the potatoes in whispered tones: *Keep growing; it's not time yet.*

I laid aside the pitchfork and dropped down to my knees. I dug with my hands, cradling each potato to wipe it of the earth dirt clinging to its sides before tossing them into the now mulch-free buckets that buried them back down two months ago.

They aren't all strong and mighty like a Russet is "supposed" to be, but the gardener worked through me to grow something in the end, something that we did together. And after the harvest buckets were hauled inside, I cried my own buckets of tears, weeping for the gardener whose harvest survives him but lies buried on the surface of the ground, visible beauty decaying, seeding, burying itself until it flowers again in its season.

ROOTS
SARA FALUGO

Living, dying, laughing, crying: these are all different acts in the great play. These are all the colors of the sheets blowing in the wind on a desert island with hills decorated in soft white buildings – curves, slopes, open windows – blue curtains billowing in the breeze. The sea is blue, a beautiful blue. The sea is warm, like a tepid bath for an infant. The roots of the trees are ancient, gnarled and wrapped around the cement blocks like the varicose veins of mother earth showing herself as enduring, lasting and there to stay.

The tree is beautiful; the roots are not. She does not care. These roots have held her trunk up for her entire lifetime. To cut them off would be to kill the tree. Mother earth is not vain. She does not care what you think of her roots. She only knows you need more of them.

"People… OH people!" she says out loud. *"Less fruit. No need to try to be so green. You will only just fall over, under the burden of all of your shiny things. The birds will peck away at your fruit. The wind will blow away your leaves. Winter will finish the job. BUT… those gnarled, twisted wholly-functional givers of life – they are what you need. Get some roots, man!"*

Slow the fuck down. Dig up all that damn cement. Plant things. Grow things. Stop looking up for salvation. It's here, right here and right now. Look around you and see what I have created for you to enjoy. This is how you atone. This is how you ground. This is how you find your way out of the whirling sea of wants.

You are here. NOW… in this moment. This is your Hero's Journey! It is your life. Your connection to your roots. Grow them. Remember the old ways.

Humanity is in the middle of its own Hero's Journey, facing almost inevitable annihilation. Some of you have left the comfort of the city to come back to the land. More will follow. The lucky will come. Others will stay, hiding behind their screens of false redemption. "I won! I got a like! I'm here now! Woo Hoo!! Look how many people think what I think!" *More fruit piling up on the sagging limbs of an almost rootless tree.* Tall, heavy, bloated with opportunity – teetering, teetering – it all could fall over any moment. Boom. Splat. Squish! And it's all gone, man.

It just takes a little wind to knock your tree over, young one. It just takes a little shake from me and everything you and your friends have built falls to the ground. You call that strength!? Me thinks not. A 100-year-old poplar tree would kick a steel reinforced building's butt in an 8.0 earthquake any day of the week.

Now, I'm not bragging. Well, maybe just a little. Chlorophyll, cellular walls and water, stronger than steel forged in the hottest fires of mankind. Who would have thought? The truth is – I was here before you and I will be here after you.

So, hero, how will it be between you and me? How will we dance together? Will you lie under my trees? Will you drink from my streams? And stop eating so much fucking meat, by the way; I really don't love all that cow shit on my face. Guess what? Chicken butt! Yeah, I have a sense of humor, as well.

So where is your savior? Where is your guru – the one who will lead you out of the darkness and into the light? Where is the one who will inspire like Jesus? Who will bring you back to me? I mean, you are coming back to me, anyway.

But let's not wait until you're dead, yeah?

I DON'T WANT TO BE ME TODAY
ASTRID VINEYARD HERBICH

I don't want to be me today
I think I'll be a tree instead.
I'll toughen my skin
And deepen my roots
And reach my arms to the sky,
I'll snack on pure light
And lean gently into the night
While staying awake with the moon.

I'll give shelter to birds
And bugs and butterflies,
Let them keep me company
While I stand here
Not worrying about the world,
Not complaining about the weather,
Not wondering what I was meant to be,
What I'm supposed to do,
Because clearly, I'm just a tree
And I'm me.

I exhale oxygen,
Turn light into lemons, limes or dragon fruit,
I talk with my roots,
Sing with my leaves,
Cry with the dew
And sigh with the wind.
I can break in a storm
And rise like a phoenix from one little shoot.
For I never forget who I am,

Who I was meant to be
And I'll always strive to grow into more,
More of me.
Taller, stronger, wiser, older,
More beautiful with every passing day
And every weathered storm.

Today I don't want to be me.
I'd much rather be a tree.

HALLELUJAH
SARA FALUGO

hallelujah
she said
as his head rolled down the mountainside
she raised her sword
while all the forest witnessed
and proclaimed in unison
hallelujah
the king is dead
there are some things
that one should not speak about
there are some things
that one should probably not even think about
let alone write about
like the slain king
with the rotting heart
and the children
who suffered under his reign

hallelujah hallelujah
in excelsis deo
she dreamt she was in the grand opera hall
and could not resist but stand up
and sing along with the choir
funerals
weddings
christenings
baptisms
brises
bar mitzvahs

confirmations
inaugurations
these are the moments
that we hold most sacred
and I must ask
just how sacred do we hold them
how sacred is the sacred exactly
and what will it take for it to be restored

she lifted her sword up high
and howled
her heart and head united
reaching beyond the heavens
she had dreamt his death
the night before
and she had written it
that morning
clarity was the only adjective needed
to describe her state of being
every curve
every line
every scent
every sound
every impulse
every movement
crystal clear
hallelujah
she proclaimed

as the women and the men gathered round
there would be no more devastation
no more domination
no more manipulation
no more lies
the children would be safe here
and the soils and trees would mend
it would require time

nonetheless
the desperation would be replaced with abundance
and the fear with unity and love
hallelujah
the king is dead

and the great mother will take her seat once again
gather incense and flowers
prepare the finest foods
a banquet shall be offered to all the earth's children

we shall sing and dance through the night
there will be three and thirty days of celebration
and three more as a final offering
the elders will care for the children
as the youthful make love in the fields
naked under the waxing moon

star children will be seeded
and will make their way to the earth in nine months' time
a seven-year cycle will be required
for the recalibration to be realized
thereafter no man, woman or child
shall struggle or strain again

seven years for the soils
seven years for the trees
seven years for the heart
seven years for the mind
seven years for the soul
seven years for the spirit
seven years for the psyche
seven years of giving
seven years of forgiveness
seven years of listening and speaking
to our bodies
to our children

to our food
seven years of meditation
of song
of prayer

no longer beseeching
a dead or decaying god
but rather
direct communion
with the mother goddess
who gives
and asks only that we receive
hallelujah
she exclaimed
as did every leaf on every tree
a new dawn had arrived
the innocence was restored

GIVING TREE

JESSE GROS

Let's dance with the plants, fancy pants.
I mean, let's get down and dirty.
Not like you are thinking – get your mind out of the toilet.
I mean, let's get down into the soil.
Let's meet the worms and the bugs.
Let's say hello to the mycelium.
Let's say howdy to the rocks and the clay.
Let's slide down the roots and twirl in the decay.

It's all about the soil, you know.
The soil is the blood of life.
The soil is the blood of all life.
Healthy soil = healthy world.

When the soil is depleted, so are we.
When the soil is depleted, the animals are depleted.
When the soil is depleted, the plants are depleted.
The animals eat the plants.
We eat the plants.
And we eat the animals.
And so on. . . .

You get it.
So when I say let's get down and dirty, that's what I'm talking about.
Let's pay attention to the dirt.
Let's give back to the dirt.
Let's give back to the soil.

"*Oh, yes!*" the ground replied.
"I would love that.

Then we could teach the people.
We could teach people about love.
We could seduce them back to the soil.
I would like that very much."

Giving tree.
Giving me.
In this moment I'm tired of giving. . . me.
I just want to be free.
And rest.

*"WELL-BEHAVED WOMEN
RARELY MAKE HISTORY."*

— Laurel Thatcher Ulrich

CHAPTER 10

Wild-Hearted Women

MY ANEMIC FEMININITY GLARES DEFIANTLY

ANJ BEE

I've enveloped myself in shadows and darkness for decades, for in invisibility, I find freedom. I'm free from the image cast upon me by the world, an image that refuses to see and believe in my humanity, in my intelligence, and in the power of my being. My father taught me one thing early: in this society, to be perceived as feminine is to be defined by weakness. And my mother taught me that to be feminine is to be a target, but beauty is a necessity for survival. And so, I pushed my femininity deeper and deeper into the closet, purely so I could survive. I marveled at the wondrous accident of my physical features. My physical beauty was always the tool, my mind the means to maneuver through the world.

But no one explained to me that masculinity and femininity lived in parallel. No one explained that the forced invisibility of the feminine was the illness of a masculine-obsessed society – a society terrified of emotions and softness. I wrote in the dark, painted in the dark, danced in the dark, thrived in the dark. I lived in a space where my feminine would not be judged, and I could be free.

My aunt defied that principle. She refused to stuff her femininity in a closet. She loved whom she loved. She expressed herself as she chose, whether masculine or feminine. And her strength moved mountains. Her strength drew a whole tribe of Afghans to the pueblos of New Mexico, because she refused to relinquish her hippie lover and conform to Kabul society. I envied that strength, that ability to choose a path without remorse, until I was forced to. But the masculine paved the way for a feminine that still lay anemic in the back closet, terrified of being revealed, preferring invisibility.

Then I met him. Finally, someone who provided me with that safe place where my masculine could nap on the sofa, while my feminine could quietly emerge and sip on a cocktail. A place where suddenly both sides of my being could be quietly present without having to retreat. My feminine grew more vibrant in that space. She stopped looking like a ghost and his affection brought a rosy tinge to her gaunt cheeks.

Yet, in that space, she still felt judged. She felt the only way to be sexually-valued was to be dominated. And she would've loved it, if one crucial component hadn't felt missing all those years: intimacy – that sense of someone loving every fiber of her skin, wanting to experience every molecule of her being – to be taken to places neither of her had ever experienced.

And then he shifted, and along with the shift came judgment. She slowly retreated to the closet again, hoping this was all a bad dream. Hoping she wasn't experiencing love and acceptance for the first time, just to have it ripped away. Where was that soft hand she skipped down Tottenham Court Road? What could she possibly have done to have destroyed that? Haunted by confusion, by the agony and the shame of loss, she shrank. Perhaps shrinking could restore her love, and in her smallness, he would feel more powerful.

Shrinking gutted her, an energetic bulimic, vomiting out the last bit of life force, praying it would make her more digestible. Her anemia returned, and with it, the pallor, the gauntness that long-haunted those cheeks. He couldn't see that the form he slept next to had lost her life force, her femininity. The radiance that echoed through her laughter had vanished, hiding in the back closet because they couldn't stand being judged any longer. On her birthday she collapsed, and he placed those haggard bones in the dustbin behind the building.

In doing so, he freed her to return to invisibility, to feel her own limbs again, and to embrace all the twinkling lights and shadows that the evening glow of the neighborhood neon lights sprinkled across her face. He broke her open, so she could unabashedly charge out of that room and feel the bare light on her naked face without the shame of walking through this craggy, jarring world unloved. For what did it matter when the beauty of nature could caress your face and enliven your senses through the gentle murmurs of the wind? The madwoman ran down the street unmasked, relishing her freedom – for only the mad are truly free.

IT WAS A COMING-OF-AGE MOMENT

IONA RUSSELL

What is that moment? You know that moment that you hold onto with the grip of fingernails hanging off a bleak and blistery cliff? I beg you to be honest with yourself, even if not with me. What is that moment that stands out for you as the most pivotal in your unfolding in those 'most formative years'?

Is it a moment of lost innocence, trauma, trepidation, and turmoil?
Or is it an instantaneous, riveting, excitement-filled adventure at warp speed in an open top Cadillac, the wind blowing through your bones, heading headfirst with no net along the highway to your city of sin?

When I came of age, was it too soon, or was it too late? It snuck up on me like a stolen cloak. There was nothing particularly noticeable that marked an end or a beginning. It was a fun and slippery slope away from my broken-hearted, tormented, self-destructive being, and into the arms of vibrant visual stimulations, sticky floors, laughter, dancing, fake IDs, and spectacular acid tabs.

I have pockets of idealistic memories that are faint through the golden haze of disconnection and disassociation from my father, masked by my judgments, my one-woman jury, the rage, resentment, and the resistance.

You don't get to stuff me in that rigid box of conformity, not when you are filled with lies and deceit, with truths never shared, your homosexuality. No more of the 'do as I say, not what I did.' I want to color outside the lines and I want to dance until the end of time in this beautiful kaleidoscope of opportunities.

Dumpster diving, shoplifting, and peanut butter on giant vitamins.

My poor mother had no idea where I was. I'd appear when I felt like it. I'm sure she wept. She must have, especially that first time she reported me missing to the police after calling all the hospitals in anguish.

She left the revolving door always open, never closed, sitting there on her fence with bated breath, wondering which path I'd take. Would I fall down the rabbit hole and join Alice in Wonderland? Which game would I play? It was a roll of the dice as she waited... waited... and waited.

Ah, that first sweet time of my first acid tab, it was... so delicately decadent and delicious. All I felt was LOVE as I danced on rainbows, talked with the trees, jumped through stars, sang with the moon, heard crunching giant lizards and flying fantasy frogs. This was such a sweet moment. I'd never felt so safe, so loved, so connected.

I didn't have a thought for my mother, who was without even knowing it, preparing her fence post, poised and open-hearted. We both have, or rather both had, that strong Celtic beating rhythm of the wild-hearted women running through our veins, and she knew. She knew not to box me or clip my wings. She sat on her fence and waited... and waited... and waited.

My days of dancing with the acid gods in dirty hovels was blissful and short-lived, somewhat ironically, I know I'm lucky to have lived, for so many didn't escape unscathed and got stuck in hallways of addiction and death. I was a visitor passing through with the lightness of one who knows they are protected by angels.

I have always leapt without looking, secure in my innocence, and unwavering like a cat with nine lives.

My mother got down off her fence post and guided me home to roost. You might wonder what age I was and how long I danced with those acid gods of decadence and corruption. I was sixteen, and I danced till the end of time.

THE YEAR WAS 1992

BETSY GIBSON

Natalie is a beautiful woman. She has a medium build, dark shining hair that fell over her shoulders like a waterfall. When she smiled with her big white smile, everyone that saw her smiled a little brighter. Her laughter could light up the entire house. Her energy was undeniable and her ability to draw people to her was one of the many gifts given to her by the Gods.

Natalie was the daughter of an American Indian Chief of the Chumash tribe. She was deeply rooted in her family history. The tribe is located just east of Escondido, California.

When I met Natalie, she looked like an Indian princess. She was powerful and could command the room at the slightest touch. I was attracted to everything about her. I wanted to know about her family, her roots, and I deeply wanted to attend an authentic native ceremony. I anxiously waited to meet her father Ray, the Chief.

Our son, Jeffrey, fell in love with Natalie. They were so happy and began to plan a wedding. Chief Ray came to our house. To my ridiculous surprise, he was just a regular man. I had imagined him grand and compelling, like his daughter. He had long hair, braided with a small feather in it. But Ray had no charisma; Ray had no joy, Ray was there to hand us his daughter. He asked only to burn sage at the wedding and had no other questions or thoughts that he chose to share with us.

All our children were excited about the upcoming wedding. Natalie spent more and more time with us. Her beautiful energy was always available. There was nothing that seemed inauthentic about her love of life and the love for all of us.

The day came to meet Barbara, Natalie's mother. She was a polar opposite of Natalie. She was bitter and mean. I could not understand where Nat found her beautiful energy, coming from the two humans that felt so lifeless and without love. She, too, asked no questions or had any requests about the wedding. She, too, seemed to just be handing her daughter over to our family.

Natalie loved all our children and, in turn, they all loved her. It was as if she was meant to be a part of us.

Natalie and Jeffrey had a beautiful wedding filled with love and laughter. I remember it because I have pictures. I have very little of my own memories of the event because it took place a week after my mother passed away. I had to fly home from being with my dad to help put on a wedding for them.

Jeffrey and Natalie had two beautiful babies, Jeffrey III and Jaynee Ray. Those were our first grandchildren, and I can tell you grandchildren are an amazing thing to love. With grandchildren, you really only need to love them. They have parents to teach them about life. And love we did, we spoiled them, all of us. Jeffery has five younger siblings and all of them loved their new nephew and niece.

Years later, drugs came into Jeffrey and Natalie's life. Drugs led to dishonesty, which led to cheating, which led to separation. Natalie no longer shined. She couldn't breathe. She came to me crying so often. It broke my heart. Her beliefs were that she had married not just our son, but our whole family. She felt like she would always be my new daughter. Nat was my daughter in so many ways, but blood lines run thick in difficult times. Eventually, she decided to move to Arizona and take our two grandchildren to live with her mother. While it broke our hearts, it was what she needed.

Chief Ray was removed from his hierarchical position and decided he, too, would move to Arizona. He moved Nat and the kids in with him. The children began to feel love again. Ray had softened with this decision and became the main father-figure to the children.

Natalie went deeper and deeper into drugs and prostitution. The children were often left with Ray for weeks at a time. As Ray's health began to fail, little Jeffrey and Jayne had to handle all the chores and responsibilities. They often had chips and soda for meals. There was no one to help them with school. As their lives continued to deteriorate, Natalie moved from one man to the next, wherever she could find meth and shelter. Her body withered to a skeleton.

Ray passed, and it destroyed the children. I went to be with them and was shocked by the things I witnessed. Natalie would not let me help them, except with the finances.

Natalie married one of the men in her life, and they moved the children into a trailer. The trailer park was filled with drug dealers and criminals of all sorts. The children lived in fear and hunger.

When Jeffrey died, I flew them all out here for the services and most of our family did not recognize Natalie at all. She mourned the life she was unable to create without Jeffrey.

When Natalie returned to Arizona, she quickly got pregnant. She had a little boy named Anthony. Jaynee loved that little brother like he was her own baby. Natalie immediately began taking drugs again, leaving Anthony with Jaynee to care for him.

When Anthony was two, he pushed open a sliding screen door and fell into a swimming pool. He died.

Natalie was crushed beyond repair.

Natalie is still alive, living with all her thoughts and the ghosts of her past. Her only living thought is how to get her next fix.

Where did her spirit go? Our beautiful Natalie who could light up the room with her sheer energy.

ONE OF THE LAST WILD WOMEN

SARA FALUGO

she was one of the last wild women
and she went by many names
and her face sometimes appeared more round
and at other times more square
and her skin too
tended to change in shade
the one constant was her strength
her body lean
her soul tendinous
her spirit resilient
she knew how to dance with the winds
as they moved to and fro
she knew how to speak to the waters
ride the currents
and befriend the tides
she was one of the last wild women
determined to give birth
to the many that would follow
in her footsteps
knowing that in order to truly be wild
they would have to stray
to rebel
to leap into the unknown

yet she would at least
pave the way
clear a path
to prepare them

for their respective journeys
the path would be a labyrinth
a mandala
a choir
a full orchestral suite

she knows the wild
like the trees know the sun
she undresses each evening
and runs naked
through the fields
through the forests
through the rainfall

sometimes she runs
until her feet are bruised and bleeding
not simply for the joy of it
nor solely for the pleasure that she receives
she runs to keep the wilds wild
to harness the unharness-able
and anchor the un-anchor-able
to the collective consciousness
lest art become an oddity of the past
reduced to an unintelligible
impractical
means of passing time
lest all creativity rot and crumble
and its carcass left for the vultures of the over-culture
lest religion have its way
and every little girl
grow into a subservient
well-adjusted
shadow of a woman

she runs and howls
and lights fire to the occasional village
simply as a reminder

of the lightning that resides
within the heart and soul
of every flesh and bone born
goddess of the earth
a reminder of the passions
that exist between the heart and the thighs
that should never grow hungry
or be subject to shame

she runs
she howls
she dances with the darkness
fearless
she breathes in the rot
the distortion
the domination
manipulation
the war machine

in every possible sense of the word
she dances with the dark lord
tango
she breathes his sordid intention
into her every cell
and laughs
as the emptiness
that is the substratum
makes love to love itself
and receives the darkness
like a mother receives a newborn babe
to her breast

she runs
she howls
she dances
she weeps
and the skies weep with her

as hurricanes make their way across countries and continents
all the world is her playground
a wonder
a mystery
a cemetery
and a garden

through her weeping
humankind is reminded
of the waters of the womb
and of the sacred birth canal
and a rebirthing is extended
to all who wish to run wild too
she was one of the last
but also the first
the first of a new tribe
whom in truth would birth her
just as she would birth them

she runs
she howls
she dances
she weeps
she paints a mural across the sky
in crimson
in violet
in golden hues
she paints the goddess
for all eyes to see
and she sings out her name
for all ears to hear

she trusts the process
even as the earth trembles and quakes
beneath her feet
she bows to the sun
and kisses the moon

and makes love to the likes of Shiva
as he sets another world aflame
until only ash remains
and she feels a stirring
a cohesion
a gathering
a redemption of sorts

when out of the ash
her wings begin to form
with a luminosity unfathomable
like the thousand suns of the Gita
her eyes rest upon the body of Brahman
and divine copulation is all that is left to be experienced
including every possible ache
every possible joy
every possible longing
yearning
desire and pain
everything imaginable
and everything yet to be imagined
and she takes her first breath
opens her eyes
and falls in love with the unknowing

I COME FROM THOSE WHO WORKED WITH THEIR HANDS

MARTHA JEFFERS

It takes the best of us to create a world destined to fall into the pure essence of Love. Some work with their hands, some with their hearts, and others with their minds to arrive at that gentle place of homecoming – Love itself.

We forget, as we arise from our dreams, that life is only always present for us. And we forget, often! We stay connected to and controlled by the everyday habits of doing, of pursuing an imaginary goal, the anticipated end of the road. Filled with timelines, expectations, lists, shoulds, coulds, and obligations, we meander an unforgiving road of never-present-ness!

My ancestors worked with their hands to bring food to the table to feed many mouths. The Abuelos followed the strings of opportunities and drew from the rich and fertile soil of creation.

Abuelo Luis Alberto used his hands to make beautiful and fashionable men's suits and winter coats. His tailor shop was well-established. Men from wealthier families came to him for their special garments. The suits were elegantly-made to have a strong, masculine presence. Old pictures show him wearing his favorite dark brown or black, single-breasted, two or three-buttoned jackets. His suits fit him well, giving him the illusion of being taller than his 5'6" frame. His hands, and those of my mother and his daughters, were the creative tools used to make garments bestowed to men of class. The tailor's craft and his creations were his labor of love.

I come from those who labored.

My Abuelo Leonidas used his hands to herd cattle, horses, and sheep, to plow, plant, and harvest. Those calloused hands milked the cows, branded the cattle, sheared the sheep and mended the fences. He was in love with what the earth provided to feed his family of thirteen. My father spoke of how Abuelo Leonidas would stand for long periods of time, reviewing and observing the fruits born from the sweat of his brow and the strong tanned muscles of his arms and back.

Both Abuelos left a legacy of deep commitment to their passions. One crafted from beautiful wools or tweed, while the other tilled the soil with great care and wisdom. Their values were that of strength and perseverance. Their heads, hearts, and hands led their quests to make a difference in their world.

Neither my children, nor I, run a plow or make elegant clothing. We stare at a screen and call it "labor." The fruits of our labor are found in paper files or in iCloud storage, the light of the computer screens softened by the use of blue lenses. We spend our lives in the wild caverns of the internet. Somewhere in the ethers lie our creative muses waiting to be discovered.

Some work with their hands, some with their minds. My work is healing hearts. I have chosen to work with the people, silently sitting with those in their time of need, listening.

THERE SHE WAS

MICK BREITENSTEIN

I closed my eyes and lay on my makeshift meditation set up. The glow of the computer and the roaring pellet stove were the only sources of light in the room. Temperatures outside were well-below freezing. Inside this studio/office we created, it was a challenge to keep it warm enough to not notice how cold it really was outside. Two space heaters at my feet struggled to keep my toes warm.

I wanted to blow off the night, not show up, not breathe. But there I was. I was tired, not in the mood to meditate. I knew I wouldn't go deep. I planned to breathe casually, to listen to Jesse's calming playlist and, at the very least, release some tension in my body. Days of shoveling snow and trudging back and forth to our Airbnb campsites carrying firewood had worn me down.

"OK, let's start the breath." I jumped right in, letting go of my thoughts, concerns, and resistance. There's always a little of that with me whenever I'm doing something that is good for me. I allowed my breath to move gently from my belly to my chest and exhaled fully until I had nothing left. I was aware of the music and Jesse's voice that came in from time-to-time with encouragement and love.

My breath naturally deepened, and I had a flashback to a time I participated in an Iboga medicine journey over a long weekend. My breath moved naturally through all of my chakras, and I could feel it move all the way up to my third eye – a point that usually takes a lot more effort to reach. I asked the plant medicine mother to guide me. Boom! A vision appeared squatting at my feet. My eyes were still closed and it was as if I could see above myself. A full-figured African woman was at my feet. Her dark skin had white bands painted around her arms, legs, and torso. She wore some sort of loincloth and a simple headdress made of grass and straw. She was doing a slow, rhythmic dance at my feet. Calm and easy. In a nonverbal communication, I asked her what she was doing. "Protecting you," she responded. I felt it. I felt the calm and ease. No fear. Actually, I felt nothing. Almost like a void. Clean, I felt clean.

"Who are you?" I asked. And the answer rang in my mind, *Isha.* "Isa?" I asked. *ISHA!* Isha – got it. I wasn't familiar with this name. Perhaps I've heard a reference to it before? Isha. At the end of the session, almost all physical tension had left my body. I wasn't freaked out about this experience. I've had visions and thoughts, dreams before, but never like this without any assistance from some plant medicine or psychedelic drug. This all occurred with the breath and coming into the session with very little desire to "go deep."

When I returned to the house, I grabbed my laptop and googled ISHA. In Sanskrit, she is the "one that protects." Maybe I already knew that, but not that I had remembered. In Arabic, isha refers to a night prayer. Both meanings seemed to ring true on this night. Throughout my life, I've overlooked or dismissed these types of experiences. Chalking it up to figments of my imagination or taking information that was already in me – forgotten, then oddly regurgitated at a future date. But this one was clear, super clear. Without any exterior interventions, no drugs, and I wasn't even breathing that deeply.

IT'S ABOUT THE WOMEN
MARTHA JEFFERS

She lay still in the quiet of the room, gently breathing with her eyes closed. I watched over her, outlining every detail of her face with my eyes. Her skin was a pale luster, as thin as rice paper, and I could see the light blue venules through its transparency. Her fine nose was well-defined and her eyes occupied the deep sockets that formed her face.

Then I noticed her hands, small for a four-foot-ten-tall woman, with beautifully-manicured and painted red nails, the color she so loved. Her gentle hands were adorned with the wedding ring given by her beloved, as testimony of their fidelity; those hands rested lightly on her chest, moving with the rhythmic dance of her breath.

I watched silently. Tears flowed down my face. She was my mother – mi Madre – the woman I had known for seventy-four years of my life and the storm that caused me to tumble into the abyss so often. I craved for her to accept me fully and take me into her arms.

I took the evening watch that night, at times from afar, at other times lying beside her, holding her close to ward off the fear of the coming unknown: the piercing of the veil, when the last Amen would be spoken.

She was one of the strong-willed, opinionated, and dedicated women of our matriarchal tribe. Her life was all about the women in her clan – the missteps, the adultery, the venial sins, the greater sins, the shame, the control, the right and wrong of it all. Forgiveness was lost between the rancor and the insatiable bickering about matters of the heart.

It's about the women, their lives wrapped in dark shawls, hiding the scars of their past. Often unaware of their own brilliance, they were consumed by the patriarchal norms of their time.

My life has been all about the women: the ones I would never allow to get near, the women I did not trust, the too-feminine and the too-masculine, the women who embraced victimhood and the ones who fought like hell to climb the ladder to the top, the women who appeared over and over again, serving as my mirror and my envoy to do my shadow work, and the women who have thrust me into recovering the rejected parts of myself.

The night after mi Madre passed, I sat in the dark and stared at her body. The life it once held evaporated into the night. Her soul journey transcended the physical world reality she once knew. She took a part of me with her, perhaps it was the struggling woman so eager to please, or maybe, it was the forgiveness I wrapped in the purple flowers I placed on her chest.

It's about the women — the anointed ones, the naysayers, the remembered ones, the obscure, the lovers, and mi Madre — unique and blessed in her own way, in her own timing.

THE PIRATE

ANJ BEE

Zazz aka 'Little Shetan:' The neighborhood smarty-pants, practical joker, and freewheeler, famous for her ability to land herself in detention and infamous for the largest liquor heist in town, for which I'll have you know, she was never caught. Excellent thief, she was! Her ability to snatch small liquor bottles off the shelves and quietly stuff them in her extra puffy coat was uncanny. Her tiny hands and overactive imagination moving at full speed were swift and almost undetectable. Theft provided an outlet for her immense intelligence. She used her creativity to find the most brazen and utterly undetectable way of breaking the law and sliding out from under the explosion she had just created, completely unscathed.

But alcohol theft was just one of her many talents, as she had also mastered the art of sneaking in and out of people's houses, especially her own, through every tactic imaginable: climbing through vents, scaling up the side ladders of buildings, dangling off balconies and swinging through open windows. She prided herself on her abilities, but conveniently ignored that she was most likely never caught, because the house she most frequently broke into was her own.

Why didn't she simply walk through the front door, you might ask? Well, she could have. But that would've forced her to encounter her manic-depressive alcoholic mother. Returning home empty-handed without any liquor bottles would've unleashed a hell that little seven-year-old Zazz would have to tame. So much simpler to scale up the side of the wall, through her narrow window, and into the safety of her bedroom, where she could watch the blinking fairy lights make colorful patterns on the ceiling, and tell her toy horses stories of brave, heroic warriors who happily made their home in the mountains. But for Zazz, bravery, heroism, mountains, and especially home, were romantic and unfamiliar illusions. Still, dreams are the mechanism through which our souls survive even the darkest night.

What she didn't realize until she finally escaped from that house a decade later, was that she knew one thing above all else, survival. She had lived to fulfill two goals: keeping her mother sedated and finding new creative ways to escape the house. Solitude and flickering lights were her only reprieve, the only stillness in a chaotic world that deafened her till silence and screaming were indistinguishable.

I NEVER WANT TO IGNORE BLUEBERRIES

LAURYN HILL

It was a gorgeous, tantalizing, jaw-dropping conspiracy,
Conspiracy it – with my own two eyes,
As I gaze from you to me.
Flustered, Colonel Mustard,
Spread too thin on a sandwich,
Goldfinch, yellow-bellied daredevil,
Cop a feel.

Dealt with the police twice a week.
Hide and seek from my shadow,
Who is really calling the shots, anyway?
Hit with a bullet in the chest.
I confess. I can't take it anymore,
All this stress has got me like woah!
Fame or fool's gold?
Dipped in chocolate, smother me with kisses,
I'll be your Mrs.
As long as you keep my secret safe,
Locked away in truth's tavern,
Where my nightmares go to sleep.
Peeping Thomas, the Train Engine,
Picking periwinkle poppies in Pompeii,
That one fine day,
When ashes fade away.
Blown by the wind, making new lives on other planes
Or other realities. . . .

Taking the poet's words and handing them off to the thinker.
Now that is a beautiful conspiracy.

Secretly, we speak the same language.

Maybe she hears my words and I hear her words and they sound just the same. Like the universe translates them as they swirl through the air from one mouth to the other's ear.

Like do you see the color blue the same way I do?

We both call it blue, but maybe it looks different.

Blue. I feel blue. Is that the same as the color?

I like the color blue. I'm wearing the color blue.

Yesterday I looked across the table into the blue eyes of my child who is more man than child and I thought, isn't it funny that his eyes are blue?

They say there isn't anything blue in nature. What a strange thing to say.

I mean, ignoring blueberries for a minute – although I never want to ignore blueberries – they are the best berries. But they say they aren't actually blue.

But what about the sky? That is the prototypical blue thing. And it is also the prototypical nature thing.

Clearly, THEY don't know what they are talking about.

Maybe that's a conspiracy. They are trying to convince us that they know something. That there is something to know.

Maybe there is nothing to know.

Maybe there is everything to know, but we already know it.

I know the sky. I try to see it every day. Daytime sky. Nighttime sky.

They look nothing alike.

But both are always there, one hidden behind the other.

I know both. Or maybe I know neither.

They know me, though.

Maybe they are conspiring.

Day sky and night sky meeting up for secret meetings.

Whispering to each other so that no one can hear. Or maybe they don't have to whisper because we wouldn't understand, anyway.

Conspiring to be my constant reminder. That life is vast and open.

That I am not just the thinker. She is not just the poet.

I am the lover. She is the dream catcher. I am the truth-teller. She is the dancer.

I am the ocean. She is the wind.

That blue is blue is blue is blue.

And we are the same.

WHAT I CANNOT SEE
ARMINDA LINDSAY

As a self-identifying writer (how great is it that I'm actually -- *finally* -- seeing and acknowledging myself as a writer?!), I have long-grappled with what I write versus what I want, and even need, to write. Yes, it's my story, my experience, my perspective, but there are so many people in my private and personal narrative. And all those people, at least the ones who got cast with main parts, well, how do I tell my story and not hurt, offend, shock, or push them away? Or perhaps all of the above.

Cheryl Strayed said, "The most unfortunate thing about writing a memoir is that other people exist." Ugh. The truth of that pierces me. I was just thinking yesterday how movies and television shows never show parents of the main characters in the story -- because no one lives their life like those principals live: lacking the constant judgment of others (both real and imagined), the recorded voice of your mother or priest or youth director or sibling or members of your congregation that play on repeat in your head. And when it's all five of those voices at the same time?! Help me.

I don't want to wait for the people I love to die to tell what I feel must be told. I also don't want to be the one to die with my story still in me. Someone said something about that once and there's **that** voice still lingering in my ear. Clearly I've got too many voices besides my own and it's awfully crowded up in here. Send help. Seriously.

Anne Lamot said that "You own everything that happened to you. Tell your stories. If people wanted you to write warmly about them, they should have behaved better." And that's laughable; it is. But here's the thing, my people (at least) don't believe they've behaved badly! Quite the opposite, in fact. They stand tall on their towers of righteousness because it gives them the best vantage point to peer down at me in my lowly, wayward life of choices that put me squarely in the seat of wrong-doing, or wrongs-done, all according to them and the internalized teachings they silently prey upon all those around them.

And all this downward glancing and judgment-casting is done insidiously; they do not know they are doing it. And bless them, I get it. Except when I don't. When it comes around again after you believe you've traversed the forest, seen all the trees, felled in conversation the ones that were standing solidly between you, borne your own heart's aching and resuscitated yourself all in their presence. . . . and yet.

Two days ago my almost 25-year-old (old enough to know her own mind, her own heart and her own choices) daughter relayed a conversation she had just had with my mother. My mother who is not yet old enough to know that she (my mother) and we (my daughter and I both) are all old enough, okay enough, loved enough and divine enough to know and to choose from that knowing how to live this one beautiful life we are each living.

The blow her words deliver is meant to hurt us into changing our choices, or at the very least penitently acknowledge her rightness and our wrongs. But those choices of ours are actually the liberation from the fear-mongering she long-ago internalized as the language of a harsh and judgmental god, which language has been cultivated and refined over a lifetime of not choosing for herself, but of having delegated her choosing to the god and the men surrounding her, who speak on his (god's) behalf .

"You were raised better than that," must be a cry sounding from deep within herself and echoing back into her own heart's remembering. She *can* own her own Self. And so can I -- respond to the cry sounding from deep within me, my heart's constant prodding, pressing and preparing me to write my story because I have raised up my Self to know what's best (for me). That other people, my people, exist is what gives my existence substance.

Perhaps -- and what if -- when I tell my story I heal, inspire, delight, or draw them all closer to me? Or perhaps all of the above. We'll see; there are just too many things I cannot see. Yet.

TURNING THE CORNER
IONA RUSSELL

As I climbed out of the rusty old red car in our muddy farmyard, the most horrendous screeching noise greeted me. It was almost intolerable, like howling banshees. I had just been in the hospital for my second ear operation within twelve months.

Quite unbelievably, no one realized I had been deaf all my young life. I entered this world with the umbilical cord wrapped around my neck, and apparently it was a bit touch and go. The specialists in London thought this might have caused the hearing issues, but they didn't really know. They reassured my parents that I'd grow out of it.

As you can probably guess, I was rather an imaginative child and I remember 'reading' the pictures to my teacher who was trying to teach me to read. I was describing in great detail what I saw with my eyes, which had been my ears for all my five formative years. This is the moment when the school realized I didn't hear unless I was looking at you.

Now, in retrospect as a parent myself, I find it quite comical and rather bizarre that my free-range-hippie-weed-growing-self-sustaining-goat-rearing-chicken-breeding-doting parents didn't pick up on this. Nor anyone else, for that matter. I was the firstborn of my siblings and on top of that, I was the crowned first-born grandchild on both sides – everyone poured love into me like velvet chocolate with sprinkles topped off with one of our home-grown deep red cherries.

Raised on a farm, it's no surprise that my first word was 'egg,' but what might surprise you is that I was allergic to eggs. Go figure. My parents discovered 'this,' but missed the fact that I could barely hear?

It won't shock you to hear that I was a late talker, and honestly never stopped once I found my voice. Having learned to speak by lip reading, I developed a speech impediment because I couldn't hear the letter S or P. So, I went to 'cool, and it was 'unny. Obviously, kind of cute for a little child to be saying.

I was a resourceful wee child with a super active imagination, frolicking freely through the mountains in Wales as my playground, with tea parties in old oak trees, fairy gatherings in the woods, and an ogre under the bridge.

Recently, I was told by an old primary school friend of mine that she used to love listening to me tell stories. I was so excited to hear all about the one she remembered the most! It had stuck with her all these years. I was such a sweet child and so I thought, "Oh, I bet it's going to be freaking adorable". . . . Um NO! Not quite.

The one she remembers to this day is a twisted tale about a knife-carrying tree that would kill you by falling on you whilst holding out the knife.

What the heck was I smoking?!

I digress, as I wandered off-topic remembering my wild wondering childhood, magically playing in the woods.

So, as our time together draws to a close, I bet you'd like to know what that howling banshee was – can you guess? Well it was birds. YEP! It was the screeching high-pitched songs from the birds!!! This does make me laugh!

Now here I am writing this for you with screaming banshees again ringing in my ears, but this time from a post-covid ear infection.

Life is funny like that.

Memories sparked with a sound reflection and remembrance of my journey from closed-off silence to songbirds whistling in the wind.

I WILL NOT GO QUIETLY INTO THE NIGHT

ASTRID VINEYARD HERBICH

I will not go quietly into the night
I will sing to the moon
And shout at the stars.
I will gather my light
And shatter the darkness,
Ripping the blindfolds from my eyes,
Hoping I'll be ready for the truth.
About myself,
The tapestry of life,
Ready to gaze at the face of God,
Ready to recognize myself:
A speck of dust
Containing everything.

I will not go quietly
But I will go willingly.

Ready to stretch beyond my skin,
And acknowledge all life as kin,
As part of me,
And I, a part of everything.

I am willing to die
To be fully alive.
I am willing to face the dark
To find the light.
I am willing to fall
To find I can fly.

I may not go quietly,
But I will try to go gracefully.
Full of grace and love and gratitude
To have been part of this magical side show,
This human farce,
Playing the roles of daughter, sister, lover, friend.
Villain, heroine, angel, devil, teacher, student.

When the lights go out
I will take a bow
And walk away from the stage.
Done playing roles,
I'll cast off my costume,
Wipe off my lipstick, take off my mask,
And walk naked into whatever truth
Lies waiting beyond the dusty curtains.

Maybe I'll meet whoever runs this show.
Maybe I'll find that no one does.
Maybe I'll find that I was the one running it all along.
Or should have, anyway.

But rather than worrying about going quietly,
Or kicking and screaming into the great beyond,
I think I'll get busy using my voice wisely while I'm here.

To heal, to soothe, to kindle kindness, rather than unrest.
To claim my voice as my own and feel the power resonating within.
I'll put my heart into my words.
I'll offer my voice to this world,
and lend my ears to listen deeply,
Letting the world resound in my silence.

So maybe I'll go quietly after all.
When all words have been said
And all songs have been sung,
When my feet are tired from dancing

And I'm ready to call it a night,
I'll take off my shoes,
Strip off my clothes,
Lie down on the ground
With a smile on my face

And let the night
And the light
Wash over me.
Quietly.

"AND THE TIME CAME WHEN THE RISK TO REMAIN TIGHT IN A BUD WAS MORE PAINFUL THAN THE RISK IT TOOK TO BLOSSOM."

– Anais Nin

CHAPTER 11

Liberation

MID-LIFE DANCE

IONA RUSSELL

Ah, the mid-life safety dance springs to mind. Do you remember the 80s band *Men Without Hats* and their song "Safety Dance"?
"We can dance if we want to
We can leave your friends behind
'Cause your friends don't dance
And if they don't dance
Well, they're no friends of mine"
I saw them play recently. Oh, no wait, that would be 3 years ago. I've lost track of time and gone into a wormhole dance these last 2 years. It's warped my concept of when things happened. It's now 2022 and I still think of last year as 2019. Ah, now I have the "Time Warp" from the *Rocky Horror Picture Show* playing in my mind. I nearly had that as my wedding dance. . . ah, I digress a decade or two. . . .

It's okay if your friends don't dance if they don't feel the rhythms dancing in their golden Gucci fancy pants. Let them go back to their white picket fences glitching in the matrix and put on their masquerade mannequin smiles and eat Betty Crocker pancakes for dinner with artificial flavours of frozen ice cream.

You, my friend, you're with me, aren't you?

Vibing and gyrating on the edge of this cliff, climbing out and climbing up higher on the ridge. Out to where bottles of beer are $9, and the pizza is an adventure in a kaleidoscopic box running free over the mountain trails, away from that beige square box of existential crisis.

You're with me, right? Cheers.

I've realized in my 52 years that I've been dancing the tango, in and out, like jack-in-the-box, jumping back and forth between pick-n-mix boxes of firefly adventures and stormy daydreams, to wanting to fit into that beige box.

Ha! But I just kept tearing out and ripping the seams with my too-muchness, my too soon, too loud, my too quirky, a little too weird, and a lot too outspoken, and way too opinionated, too forgiving, too energetic, too quiet, my breathtaking, tantalizing, and adrenalin-searching for that skydiving high.

I've never fit into that beige box. Have you? I doubt it because you're here next to me in your own fancy pants, ready to jump off and fly where the stars shine, and universal wisdom is having a tea party with the Mad Hatter. They're planning what to do with Alice as we pop another bite of magic mushroom.

Now don't be bamboozled, hoodwinked, duped or deluded into thinking I've always followed my ecstatically wild heart and blindly stepped off cliffs like the fool in the tarot without a care in the world, ready for adventure and unknown sunrises.

I have lost and found parts of myself along the way. There were times when I mistakenly gambled with the devil and sold my soul for a peanut of overly-salted, processed happiness.

Hey, have you ever sat in the peanut gallery? It sounds fancy, doesn't it? But you can't see a thing without binoculars and the view is shocking. There are no mountain ridges of adventures, no waves to ride, just B-list actors shuffling and dancing out of tune.

But hey, you are meant to be grateful for the chance to sit at the table with the likes of them. Sipping on martinis, dirty, not stirred! Following some merciless, misspelled script where everyone's talking but no one's listening. No one's cheering you on to the finish line to excel past your perceived limits. No one's encouraging you and showing you what's possible.

They want you to sit down and shut up, sipping stale beer with Debbie Downer as they tell you "No one gets out of here alive, kid" and "That's not for the likes of us; this is our lot." And it's slapped all over in oozing, putrid, beige, outdated, moldy paint.

Don't worry – spoiler alert – we do all indeed get out of here alive on an adventure, wearing our kaleidoscopic fancy pants and riding that spaceship of infinite possibilities, knowing we got this.

Buckle up ladies and gentlemen, this is going to be a fantastical, fabulous, fun ride. It's better than Alice's leap down the rabbit hole sipping Biodynamic golden bubbles of Joy from Arminda's vineyard. It is a very good year, my friends. So cheers, and as the song goes,

"We can dance if we want to…
Say we can go where we want to
A place where they will never find
And we can act like we come
From out of this world
Leave the real one far behind
And we can dance"… in our fancy pants baby.

IF YOU WANT TO MAKE AN OMELET

ASTRID VINEYARD HERBICH

If you want to make an omelet
You have to break some eggs.

And if you want to show up for your own life.
You will have to break some hearts.
Including your own.

We don't get to tiptoe toward the light.
We dance, crash, fall and stumble in the dark,
And into each other.
Bruising, scraping, breaking toward wholeness.

If we aren't willing to take ourselves apart,
How can we ever truly know ourselves?
If we never challenge other people's beliefs about who we are
Whose life are we living?

If the fear of losing love keeps us from coming into our own,
Was that love to begin with?

How can a love that has never been stretched
Ever grow strong?
It won't.
It will remain brittle,
Forever threatening to turn to dust.

Don't make yourself small for such a love.
Don't dim your light.

Don't smother your voice.
Don't stop dancing,
Or dreaming or drumming your own beat,
For such brittle love.

Challenge everyone's beliefs.
And your own.
About who you are.
Who are allowed to be.
And go looking for the one you could be
If you dared.

Go break some eggs.
Go break some hearts.
The omelets will be delicious.
And hearts may be broken open.
And find they can hold so much more
Than they ever dreamed they could.

For such is love,
That sometimes it can give us wings,
But it may also try and clip those wings,
In the attempt to keep us safe.

When love and fear entangle themselves,
They start building elaborate cages.

Cages in which they can control the light,
The food, the water, the temperature.
What you are allowed to hear and see and think.
They say: You see?
I'm keeping you safe.
You have everything you need.
Why would you ever want to leave?
No one can hurt you here.
Predators lurk outside in the dark,
But I have locked all the doors
And am keeping them away.

And all I ask of you
Is to never spread your beautiful wings and try to fly.
You can't fly.
You can't fly away from me. . . .

This is how love can be.

But when love lets go of fear
And knows itself to be eternal, unconditional,
And beyond all boundaries,
Deeper than skin and bones and feathers,
It loves nothing more
Than to see things soar.

It wants you to be free
And in your element.
It wants you to thrive and laugh
And grow beyond your wildest dreams.
And it will love you every step of the way.

This is the love I wish for you.

This is the love I wish for me.

So, let's break our hearts.
Until they are free.

OUTWARD APPEARANCES
MARTHA JEFFERS

I entered the house with a step as light as I could maneuver, but the creaking floorboards gave me away. It was close to 1:30 in the morning as I walked in, clothes in-hand, hair disheveled, and my shoes off my feet. The house was silent except for a soft snore coming from the room upstairs. I paused. I listened. My heart quickened. My husband was home! Was he not far away on his business trip across the planet?

As I made my way up the stairs, I placed each item of clothing on a step, careful not to awaken the sleeping wanderer. My palms got sweaty and my mind started constructing the stories I'd have to tell.

This was the nightmare that often flickered in the night in my restless dreams. I would awaken and feel the discomfort in my chest, tiptoeing into the living room to ponder: What did these dreams have to say and why would I awaken with so much anxiety?

There was a time when life seemed rosier than rosy and the air was filled with the fragrance of lavender love. I could sense the gentleness in my heart and the flutter in my gut whenever I saw him – it was sweet, honest. Yet, deep inside, as deep as the well found in most prairies, I felt dry and unseen. I was living a lie.

In my culture, a married woman was to be attached to the hip of her husband. Beckoning to his every need, making him the king of the castle. All attention and bestowed honor were his. Never mind the struggles she was facing. The nature of things was for the wife to maintain a peaceful, clean, happy place and, most of all, keep her man happy.

"What a bunch of bullshit!" I said to myself one day when I awakened from the illusion of "wedded bliss." The anchor was cut free and I began to drift. My belief systems dissolved as the storm clouds gathered and torrent waters fell.

I awakened to the clear remembrance of me, of the Latino woman fashioned by ancestral strings of submission and death-of-self by marriage. This awakening wasn't easy and it wasn't pretty. In fact, it was fucking hard! I walked many paths of enlightenment, crossing bridges of pain and mistrust. I opened Pandora's box to ancestral healing and confronted my parents' past.

Despite outward appearances, things on the inside looked quite different! The loving family and perfect home shielded my deep sadness of my lost identity until the day I opened my heart, my soul, and my being to do the work necessary to get her out! And out she came, full of color and enthusiasm! She danced her dance at times frantically, and at other times with peace. Motherhood, the University of Santa Monica, Portland, Half Dome, Havasupai, Machu Picchu, plant medicine, breathwork, all contributed to the discovery of an awakened Earth Mother.

Despite outward appearances, things on the inside looked quite different once upon a time.

DANCE

JESSE GROS

Dance by the fire, love.
Dance until you are no more,
Until your thoughts have burned away and become one with the stars.
Dance until your resistance has given up.
Dance until you cannot lie to yourself another moment.
Dance like your salvation depends on it.
Dance until you can feel yourself once again
Burning off the layers of sadness, grief, and disappointment that cling to your
body like moss on a tree.
Dance until you can no longer have an opinion about your government.
Dance until you can no longer hold a single grudge.
Dance until you can no longer judge.

Set yourself free, you see.
Crucify yourself in the fires of the whirling dervishes,
Skirmishes,
Within yourself,
Skirmishes in your mind.
Stop, they will say.
Stop… this is not safe.
Keep going.
Dance until your body collapses.
Dance until your personality collapses.
Dance until you have burned your synapses,
Vaporizing the old tracks of thought,
Vaporizing the old snacks of thought,
Chewing on the cud of your ancestry for eons.

Just spit that shit out.

Do it now! "Get in the choppa!"
You are not supposed to dance with your mouth full.
Didn't you know that?

Why are your shoes on?
Take them off.
What are you afraid of?
It's only blood.
Don't be so selfish.
You have quarts of the stuff.
Vampires need to eat too, you know!

SACRED EGGS
JANELLE NELSON

Nothing of great reward comes without sacrifice, right?

I'm in some sort of soul death right now and it's painful. My whole life I have skillfully managed what others thought of me. Like a chameleon I've known how to connect with each person I meet to get their approval. I collect approvals. I have a huge internal cabinet where I keep their approvals, like trophies. Last Friday I pushed the glass cabinet to the ground and watched it shatter into a million little pieces. My life's work was gone in minutes. Would Uncle John listen anymore? Cousin Julie? How about the Eastman's? Will they all think I'm crazy, that I've lost my mind? Probably.

I lost my mind in sharing my true self to the world with the hope that I would gain freedom. Freedom from having to keep a trophy case any longer. It was getting heavy. I want new furniture now.

Souls and psyches are wild, complex, delicate things. I learned at a very young age that we need to present our soul in a very tidy way. Nothing wild or complex was allowed to be shown. Tidy, straightforward and simple is the way to go. Things could get really hairy otherwise and that would be disruptive. So, no.

I'm so tired of being tidy. It's exhausting. If my truth and my insides disrupt you, so be it. I can't live tidy anymore and I hope you don't, either.

What's that saying? Oh yes, "The truth always sets you free; it might kick your ass at first, but it will set you free." I get that there is a fee to pay for a free soul and if ass-kicking is the prerequisite for freedom, then so be it.

Last week I sat with a group of my soul sisters and a wise indigenous shaman in New Mexico. We all were given a placement in a circle that represented different things: masculine, feminine, child and elder. Everyone felt connected to their placement, but had no idea what they were landing on and I was resistant to mine as we walked along the circle. I didn't know it at the time, but my placement was called the "wise woman." The shaman looked at me with knowing eyes while I struggled, "You are here because you are being asked to step into your elder now, into your wise woman." It was Friday morning, the morning of the podcast launch. I started to tear up and nodded. She took us each into deep meditation and I immediately met my eighty-five-year-old self. Gray, wiry hair. Lots of wrinkles; I loved each one. This woman gave no fucks. She sat with me, a scared forty-one-year-old Janelle. And in a very endearing way, laughed at my current stress over the podcast. She had perspective. She ushered me into the knowing that this death, this rite of passage, while huge to me now, is nothing in the span of lifetimes. We are all just little souls finding our way to authenticity. And these daily struggles? Small potatoes. I thanked her, took her spirit energy with me and completed the meditation.

I would love to say that I'm wiser now, but the truth is, I flipped someone off this morning while driving. Yep, so, there's that. I felt the shame of that all morning. I know it was from the hurt I felt from my family's lack of approval the night before. Displaced anger . . . displaced pain. Maybe we all vacillate from child to our wise self on the regular. Clearly, I do.

But the wise woman is who I want to be. She carried no trophy cabinet in her soul. She let her light shine and didn't care who her wild, untidy soul disrupts as she shares her truth. She would probably laugh at me giving the bird this morning . . . and extend grace.

I love her for that.

I'm hit with the reality that deciding to show up to my life is not just a one-time decision. Fuck, it's a daily and continuous choice.
Alright then, wise woman, let's do this.
Let's go break some more fucking eggs.
With love, of course.

ONE DAY IT WAS TRUE AND THE NEXT IT WAS NOT

ANJ BEE

One day it was true, and the next day it was not.
24 hours for life to explode, to coagulate, to morph.
The endless shape-shifting dance of time.
Devastation to triumph,
Despair to shimmering glory,
Plumpness to creaky skeletal fragility.
How the world turns in 24 hours.

In a flash, I go from hated to celebrated.
But how the fatigue has sanded my bones.
A wide-eyed corpse running through the streets,
Knowing her bones will collapse into a heap.
The clock is ticking . . . .

I power through the creaky pain,
Steam-roll over it till it dies.
But the pain always comes roaring back,
Vines around our limbs, pulling us closer to the earth,
Till we pull those roots of pain from the source,
And burn them to ash in the fire of self-acceptance.

The newness and the loss of yesterday stretched to eternity . . .
Betrayals by the beloved,
International moves each year,
Memories skipping as stress carried them away,
The heart-shattering loss of love,
The loss of family,
The loss of my dynamic sister.

Loss envelopes me everywhere,
Trapped on a tiny island that my soul would've given anything to depart.
Bullied by hyenas closing in on me,
Knives drawn, ready to show them a Pathaan's steely nerves.

The scream and the silence crescendo to the same sound, an indistinguishable echoing bellow.
I plead for my life in the stillness of the night. I plead that it vanishes into the darkness, and I can finally surrender.

How I just want to sleep and surrender the life I've built.
To climb into a tropical cocoon and sleep peacefully under a starry sky.
Instead, I enter the halls of men,
Loud rampaging elephants trample the grass they walk upon.
How I would love to lie in that grass,
Instead, I trample it with them.
I've proven myself once again.
And how dare you ask me to walk through the fire one more time!

I wear my grit as a badge of honor,
The knives of karma in my chest as evidence of my valor.
The pool of blood around me, evidence that my heart still beats,
And loudly.
I'm alive because I refuse to die.
Come trample me, you elephants.
My heart will forever resurrect itself.
It knows no surrender,
And doesn't understand death.
These gaping holes in my beating heart, the evidence.

But how I should love to lie in the grass
And flood the world with my tears.
Repressed rivers flooding the barren lands.
I have won the war.
A gaunt skeleton in oversized garments stands at the podium.
Medals celebrating madness and stubbornness fastened to my lapel.

I stare at my naked body in the mirror.
Weary bones walking through the dreary streets.
Sinews and ligaments are visible, a skeleton trudging along in oversized rags.
Blood spills from my heart through the gaping holes of heartbreak.
But shiny vibrant eyes still stare back at me, for I am alive because I refuse to die.
And my stubborn aliveness dances with its love of life,
For they both know the secret – the secret that transcendence lies in timelessness
Of the magical glimmer of twinkling nights
That radiate and pierce through this cold dark night.

Soon my bones will shatter into a million bits,
A million fragments of my heart scattered into ash.
I will achieve what I always dreamt of - timeless expansiveness.
Where I'm neither here nor there, but my soul is everywhere.
But for the moment, I shall rest.
Come find me in those tall blades of grass,
Where at last, I can stop, and be enveloped in soft silence.

EMPATHS AND NARCISSISTS
JESSE GROS

Empaths and narcissists dancing together in earth school. Each of us has something to learn. Each of us has something to give. We all came here to grow. Now for something that may be hard to swallow... There are no victims, only co-conspirators. We tend to think of narcissists as the perpetrators and the empaths as the victims. And at first look, that is what we see.

BUT, if we peek a bit below the surface, we see that things are much more nuanced. You see, us empaths, we need bullies in our lives, so we can see where we need to stand up for ourselves. Just like muscles, we need resistance, something to break down the tissue so it will build back up even stronger.

While it would be nice to just live in a softer world where we don't have to bump into these folks, it's just not reality. And so, we do our little dance together. Round and round we go, twirling on the dance floor, stepping on each other's feet, occasionally bumping into cocktail tables, sending flutes of champagne crashing to the floor.

As an empath I have come to see narcissists as the thorns on the roses of life. Each one I encounter is an opportunity to stand up for myself and see where my caring and my empathy can be more well-honed. To notice the darker side of my being.

The first rule: Your pain is not mine.
The second rule: I don't need to fix or help you.
The third rule: I am not responsible for your feelings.

This idea that I don't want to hurt anyone's feelings is a false one. Because we *can't* hurt another's feelings. We may trigger them, but their feelings are theirs. We are also not responsible for their interpretations of our words or actions.

And maybe, just maybe, if enough of us empaths learn to stand up for ourselves, the narcissists will begin to learn as well. They will learn about true empathy. Because that's their lesson: empathy is what they are here to learn. And they won't learn a thing about it if they can just jump from one doormat to the next.

I am learning to speak up for myself.

I am learning to say those hard things early in the experience so they don't snowball into more challenging ones down the road. I have compassion for these folks, and I don't need to be around them. Even if they are family, long-term friends, or if I feel some strange obligation to be nice to them, life is way too short to be nice to people who don't deserve my attention.

From a place of learning I say, "thank you narcissists." Thank you for the opportunity to stand up in myself. Thank you for the opportunity to learn to be stronger and nurture that kind of fierce love that I admire so much in others.

It's a wild lesson to learn, to see the best in others and know when it's time to move on. It feels counterintuitive, counter-feeling, and yet I know as I lean into this lesson, I can feel myself expand.

I can feel myself stretching.
It's uncomfortable.
It's all part of the wild dance.
It's all part of this thing we call earth school.

We are here to learn.
We are here to grow.
We are here to thrive.

LIVING BRAVELY
ASTRID VINEYARD HERBICH

We are brave to be living.
Brave to jump into the deep waters of this existence,
With all its riptides, stagnant shallows,
Tidal waves and endless ripples.

We are brave just for showing up,
Even if we are afraid of growing up,
Of having to face taxes, tuition,
and tensions in relationships.
Scared of losing our sense of magic
and awe of the magnitude of this world,
this galaxy, this universe,
This thing called life.

Someone wise once said,
That being brave has nothing to do
With the absence of fear,
But is the willingness to face one's fears.

And our fears are as individual and many-shaped as we ourselves are.

It can take the shape of a spider, an airplane,
A crowd of people looking at you,
Or wide-open waters.
Maybe it sounds like thunder or raised voices,
Or the silent shattering of a rejected heart.

What do your fears sound like?
What taste do they leave on the back of your tongue?
What shadows linger on your eyelids as you are trying to fall asleep?

I don't think I'm brave.
I haven't quite stood my ground and courageously laughed into the face of all
my fears.

But I have tried to reach out a hand to them, every so often.
Have tried to learn their names and get to know them,
To recognize the outline of their shadows
And their flavor in my mouth as they surreptitiously
Poison my day and my relationships.

I try to greet them politely when they show up on my doorstep,
Uninvited, once again.
I try to engage them in conversation:

So, where are you from, originally?
How long have you lived inside my brain?
What is it that you do, exactly?
Oh, so you knew my Mom and Dad?
Interesting.
Shouldn't I be charging you rent for living in my head?
Sorry, but do you have a purpose?

Fears get quite restless when they are sat down and questioned like that.
Like they're late for another appointment or something.

(Sorry, gotta go! So many more souls to torment and so little time, but no
worries
I'll see you soon!)

I think I did manage to get one or two to move out over time.
The spider-shaped one seems to be gone, haven't seen him around for a while.
The public speaking one took some convincing but rarely shows up at events,
But honestly, you can't trust her a bit, she's sly.
Every so often she will speed up my heart just for the heck of it, just to say hi,
to remind me she's around somewhere.
But a good deep breath or two is usually enough to politely escort her out.

But I know that somewhere in the mansion of my mind,
There is still a hostel of fears hidden away.
I just try and raise the rent whenever I run into one,
And hopefully, one day, maybe,
They will be on their way.

You know, I think they have a ringleader.
I have come to suspect,
That if I were to lose my fear of death,
All my other fears would follow.

If I can be ok dying a little every day
In order to be fully alive,
What else is there left to fear?

If I can laugh at my hurt ego and smilingly
Tell it to get over itself,
I've found it heals faster.
And failure and rejection don't seem
So devastating anymore.

Just one little death and so much more life to live.

I'm aging. I'm changing every day.
But I've done so all my life.
Why worry about it now?
I have become richer, fuller and more me
By living every day.
Whether they brought thunder or thoughtfulness,
Tenderness or frustrations,
Confusion or clarity,
Each day is a gift
Gently nudging me toward eternity.

To be alive is to be brave.
Do I feel brave? No.
Do I feel overwhelmed at times? Yes.

But I let the waves wash over me
And as I come back up for breath
I am grateful to be alive.
Brave or not.
I'm here.

Maybe that's enough.

LETTING LOOSE
ARMINDA LINDSAY

I was this week old when I had my first taste of alcohol. Ever. Let me do the math for you. My half birthday was on October 1, making me 47.5 years old. My unlearning, letting go, and reidentification of Self (as told me), into Self (as I create and choose me) has now occupied a decade, plus at least four years more. There have been a handful of milestone moments in this – my unlearning phase of the life I'm living.

If I provide you a checklist it might be easier for you to follow along and keep track.

- ✔ Stop wearing the clothes I've been told to wear

- ✔ Start wearing sleeveless tops, shorts, and skirts above the knee

- ✔ Stop weekly attendance at Sunday service

- ✔ Breathe deeply when church members openly judge me and call my attention to my sins

- ✔ Actively engage in debriefing conversations with my daughter about what she is being told and taught and wonder if the entire world might actually stop spinning if we walk away entirely

- ✔ Remind myself my daughter's accusation of *me wearing a bikini is a sin* is not my daughter's thought but one planted in her by someone else

- ✔ Imagine, again, a world in which we live without the weight of what is expected, required and obligatory

- ✔ Show up to therapy and talk out loud to the sofa across from mine using language I was never taught correlated to marriage, relationship, and love. Words like *rape* and *sexual abuse*

✔ See that healing a wound I didn't know I had will require behaving in a way I didn't know I was allowed and I will, like Eve, sin in the eyes of others (but in my own eyes, heart and soul understand the necessity of knowing I am not broken) and be known by a man

✔ Go DEEP with the guilt of my learned bad behavior, spend countless sleepless nights praying and pleading with my God for forgiveness, understanding, and desperation that He not take my daughter from me, that the earth remain intact and not swallow me whole, that my sins not be as visible as Hester's scarlet letter

✔ Drop therapy for making me feel worse on the other side of a session on the couch than progressing or understanding anything

✔ Know in my heart that constantly revisiting the past is no way to create a future

✔ Go back to school. Sure. Get a master's degree in Spiritual Psychology because that's the obvious thing to do

✔ Reinvent God and my entire relationship to Him. Wow. He is so much bigger than I ever understood before

✔ Say "FUCK" for first time

✔ Recognize that using the words SHIT, FUCK AND DAMN take practice to incorporate into my vernacular — for others' comfort and my own

✔ Send my daughter to university in a city too far from my heart

✔ Begin what may be a lifetime of grieving the vacancy left in her absence, a void from 18 years of daily loving no longer with me

✔ Sell my home and downsize into a city that is too small to hold me

✔ Move across the country to check off others' dream of LA living that was never my dream

✔ Keep dreaming

- ✔ Survive LA

- ✔ Complete my graduate studies

- ✔ Fall in love with being with mySelf

- ✔ Reconnect and reinvent relationship with my brother, be fully and truly seen by him — the first and only member of my family to reach out to me for understanding, for loving and being together by choice

- ✔ Receive my dad's cancer diagnosis with a criss-cross applesauce move back across the country, carrying and keeping only that which fits into the Civic. Nothing else matters.

- ✔ For the first time in my 47 years come home as mySelf, wholly, fully in my loving

- ✔ Live simply as the presence of Love, loving both my parents exactly where, who and why they are. I am Love. And I am loving every single minute.

- ✔ Meet Grief again and in an entirely new way on June 29

- ✔ Take a deep breath and taste a mimosa because the earth won't swallow me, my mom still loves me, my daughter will always be mine and I will keep creating me. With love. As love. Only always.

A BOTTLE OF WHISKEY

ASTRID VINEYARD HERBICH

A BOTTLE OF WHISKEY,
A NEW LOVER
AND A CAR CRASH.

Tropical thunderstorms,
Bloodthirsty sharks
And magical mushrooms.

Fights with your mother,
Things you said to the dead,
Words spoken in anger
Never to be unsaid.

A sadness so dark you can feel it on your skin
And taste it on the back of your tongue.
A song unsung.

A love so deep it tears at your heart.
Whiskey, lovers, and car crashes.
These are the things that rip you apart.

Crystal clear water,
Dear, familiar lovers
And the smell of rain in the air.

Apple pie fresh from the oven,
A smile from a stranger,
A poem placed gently into your palm.

A walk on the beach,

A swim in a lake,
An honest talk long-overdue.

A good book and some tea,
Your mom's "Goodnight, sweetheart."
My dog rolled up on the couch next to me.

A love so deep it heals every pain,
Pie, poems, lovers and lakes,
These are the things that put you back together again.

No matter how broken.
I can be mended.
With poems and pie and time and tea.
Even shark bites will heal.

So, I won't be afraid.
Of loving and crashing.
Too much whiskey and sad songs.
I'll let the thunderstorms wash over me
And I'll cry and dance in the rain.

For I know there is always something out there
Waiting to put me back on my feet again.

REMEMBER WHY WE'RE HERE
ANJ BEE

We're here at the beginning of time,
At the beginning of this now,
For this moment is the beginning of time.
We stand at the precipice of our own making,
Leaping to a branch we have yet to envision,
The moment of your reckoning.
To love that which you fear most – Freedom.
Your crucifixion and resurrection.
Your burden and my blessing.
For only those who stretched every parameter of their being,
Flirted with the edges of decency,
And extorted every opportunity with the purest intentions,
Only she can call herself a pirate.

I am me.
A vigilante.
An impostor in a delicate society,
Yet society's most exuberant guest.
For who enjoys a transient state more than she who knows it's indeed transient.

You fool.
You silly fool, attempting a rare form of kidnapping.
That form induced by consent and coercion.
How dare you try to seduce me into your domesticity?
And expect me to remain permanently.
As if I could ever succumb to suffocating complacency,
Banish loneliness and embrace the chains of placid comfort!

Complacency deadens my nerve endings,

Till the blood begrudgingly crawls through my veins.
I wear my freedom as my badge of honor,
Forged through continuous deaths and rebirths,
Of the stubborn refusal to surrender my soul to a gilded cage,
Warm outstretched in your left palm, starvation in the right palm.

I take that which you rammed down my throat and I'll raise you a few times over.
The grenade of uncertainty in my left palm, sudden death in my right,
With five seconds to choose your fate.
Tick Tock, Tick Tock. . . .

I stand at the ledge as you walk towards my door,
Hat in hand,
Softly murmuring a prayer that has sat on my lips for five years.
But a prayer perhaps never to be answered, as I lean into the scars of pain-induced wisdom,
Seared into scars from so many neglectful moments.
Traversing the caverns of longing,
Pierced by stalactites and stalagmites,
Trudging through the putrid stench of shame.
Yet there I stand, hat in hand, with a prayer ready to spring from my lips.
I will die at the stake of hope,
For hope is all I have left. Hope is all I am.

We cross that bridge one last time,
Bathed in the light of our love,
Of a love that always was,
And still echoes through eternity.
Another dimension of the timeless soul,
Whether crossing through this city,
Or crossing the portal to another life,
Across that bridge I walk
With you by my side.

Forever we shall walk this way,
Each moment, so sickly sweet,

Till the dreary nights claim my bones,
And the wind howls and bellows through me.
Till the howl and silence fuse into one.
My hollowed chest but an empty cavern,
Searching for a heart it once held close.
An alien floating through the universe,
Where pain births ghouls no longer of this planet.
Our only tie to this earth is the bridge to our deepest happiness,
Where love echoes in our footsteps,
As we traverse the bridge of time.

And here I still dream
Of you being by my side.
When we traversed a bridge to nowhere,
Leaping and dancing for pure joy,
That our limbs could indeed do such a thing,
And leap into the freedom of love.
That love once again echoes through eternity
As we spring in tandem across that bridge.
And forever our souls shall dance this way
as we traverse the world in time,
Until that moment I find your body again,
and we cross that bridge side by side.

"ALL THINGS MUST COME TO AN END, SO THAT NEW THINGS CAN BEGIN."

– Dalai Mama

CHAPTER 12

New Beginnings

END
ASTRID VINEYARD HERBICH

It's not the thing that ends that mourns.
It's the one witnessing the ending.

It's we who are asked to let go,
We who have loved,
We who are not ready to move forward
Into change, who suffer.

The thing itself has already moved on,
But has not taken us along.

So we stand, alone in our grief,
In our fear of an unknown future,
Stuck in our idea of how things should be
And our illusion of permanence and control.

But Entropy will come knocking on all our doors.

And we will be in our pajamas and slippers,
Teacup in hand,
And she will waltz right in,
Without waiting for an invitation,
And turn our world upside down.

Insisting that it's time to move on.
Right now.
PJs, slippers, tea and all.
Ready or not, here we go.

And as you walk, stunned, out into the storm,

And the wind whistles through your brain,
Blowing away your habits,
Your belief systems,
Your false sense of security,
She will bring you to your knees,
And make you, unwillingly, surrender to chaos.

But lying there, drenched, shaken and barely able to breath,
Eventually, you may notice a small patch of blue sky
Opening up, right above you.

Then the whistling slowly subsides,
Then the dust settles on your skin,
And everything around you,
Having done its worst,
Comes to an exhausted and complete calmness.

And as you pick yourself up from the dirt,
and take in the wide and empty landscape all around you,
You see a new slate, like an offering.

And amidst all that emptiness,
One thing stands,
Red and shiny and new:
A door.
Made just for you.

Entropy has carried you
All the way to Fate's doorstep.

Now all you need to do
Is walk through.

Thank God, or the Universe, or Entropy or Fate,
But somehow, these unexpected doors always
Show up for you.

Some may be harder to see than others.

Maybe you'll stumble upon six at a time,
And then will have to choose.

No you will never know what's on the other side
Before you've walked through.
Where would be the fun in that?

Trust chaos to plow the way,
To blow away the walls of limitation,
And create space for all the gifts
Fate has dreamed up for you.

And when it's time,
When we have locked ourselves once more
Into ivory towers of limited beliefs and attachments,
Entropy will show up on our doorstep again,
Riding on a storm,
Whistling a song,
And tear our towers down,
Joyfully, gleefully, relentlessly.

Reminding us with a patient smile and kind eyes,
That this is what we signed up for.

We were never going to get to keep anything.

Naked we arrived
And naked we will leave.

We only get to take what we can carry in our hearts.

I HAD IT ALL
ARMINDA LINDSAY

Is there someplace where it is said, *First the burning, then the shining?* Maybe that place is only in my head, so I'll go ahead and claim it as my own unoriginal thought. Viktor Frankl definitely said, "What is to give light must endure burning."

I had it all. I mean I really had it all. And I burned it right to the ground. No regrets now but certainly not the case during that 10-year combustion phase.

Burning – my burning. It's interesting in retrospect.

What is the all I had and consciously chose to burn? I was given the "keys to the kingdom," as it were: all the knowledge — the literal knowing — of right versus wrong, good versus bad, purpose versus pleasure. I was handed the script for living (if you consider the accumulation of good marks while living being tallied toward the greater reward to be awarded *after* dying as "living"), told which part was mine and memorized my lines long before the director said I needed to be off-script. I've always been an overachiever like that.

The all I had was the idyllic description taken straight from the script — it was scripted perfection, honestly, and I never needed or asked for a line prompt; it's as if I was born to play my part. Is that type-casting? (Something to look into.) I was a natural: the embodiment of method acting. I read all the books, answered all the questions, studied my mentors' every moves, and demurred and deferred to every single man just on-cue. I said Yes when my body would have had me say No.

My relationship and relatedness to all the other players was strictly professional; I kept it that way intentionally and without realizing it. I could not break character for fear of being recast and replaced by someone else willing herself to perfection. I was perfectly obedient.

Until I wasn't.

One line at a time, scribbled on and removed from the script, I set a little match. I never burned the entire script; it would have caused too big a flame and would have attracted too much attention. I would have been kicked out of the cast in front of everyone. That burning would have burned me, burned others close to me. I was never an inflictor of wounds, not knowingly. I chose to burn from the inside out instead. My wounds were my own to tend. But their infliction? Whose were those?

I recently read an account of the very young Judy Garland on the set of *The Wizard of Oz* and I understood how large a Metro-Goldwyn-Mayer studio loomed above and around her in the real-life body of a Mr. Louis B. Mayer managing and controlling her every move, her very voice, touching all aspects of her performance as if it were for him, alone.

Personal performance notes I took to heart: "No man, when he hath lighted a candle, putteth it in a secret place, neither under a bushel, but on a candlestick, that they which come in may see the light" (Luke 13:11). I understood I was meant to give light, not to hide it under a bushel or under a marquee not of my own making. I slow-burned my all to the ground because my on-demand rote performance wasn't life or light-giving.

First the burning, now the shining. I'm taking my encore performance: I was burned to shine.

THIS AIN'T NO FAIRYTALE
IONA RUSSELL

Shhhh. Let us begin. No throwing popcorn from the cheap seats.
The curtain rises and the lights come on.

Cue the song playing in the background (of my mind), The Pogues' *Fairytale of New York.*

This past year has been the best and the worst of years. I hear the careening, crooning, candy cane musical notes of yesteryear across the airwaves from the other side of grace and valor, with a scattering of dirty ol' smog tinged with the Pogues' gritty yellow-stained teeth – the too much, too sweet, too yellow eggnog sugar song – waves of sea sickness as teeny boppers gyrating like pirates to out-of-tune guitars wishing for a better start next year. . . .

What did they wish for?
What did you wish for?

Are you sipping the Kool-Aid of Transcendental Actualization: Health, Wealth, Love, and Freedom, with whimsical whispers of wonder and awe, adventures over land and through levels of consciousness? This will be the year that I – that we – will be as one.

Oh, just pass the joint on dude.

Or are you of the perceived nouveau riche? Those luxury bunch of misfits with molasses-caked fool's gold oozing with self-prescribed success as seen on Instagram – a new shiny car, a Rolex watch, a mansion in the hills with a pool no one uses, and a painted-on grin just for the cameras. . . .

Oh, go on, pass the cocaine-encrusted mirror along my friend.

"You were handsome
You were pretty
Queen of New York City
When the band finished playing
they howled out for more,"

What was it you wanted more of?

I have danced in-between the liminal spaces of the hippie bandwagon and the girl boss gang. Jeeesh, I needed cocaine for that. I'll share a secret: cocaine was my vice back in the day, but there were no Rolodexes in sight.

Who decided which camp you could be in, should be in, would be in, or even wanted to be in. . . ???

This year I have been in *no camp* at all.

And I couldn't even dress myself at the beginning of the year. I kid you not! I hurt my back so badly, my son had to dress me on Christmas day as I waited on a legal high of narcotics being prescribed to me. This will be one Christmas I will never forget. EEK... that *he* will never forget.

It took me five weeks before I could put on my own socks. I lived lying down with frozen peas on my back and a bottle of codeine at my side. FUCK! Not this. Not me. Not now. I am not going to go out like this.

This was NOT the deal I signed up for!

I've been misled by the dodgy car salesman, self-subscribed fallen Angel of Opportunity. To get old and crippled before I had lived louder and lighter, and carved out a piece of heaven in my own heart.

It may not sound like much to dress yourself, but let me tell you, I celebrated from on high with the Angels when I managed this all by myself. Have you ever longed for something so simple, so normal, that the gift of it is sweeter than all the nectar of the gods?

This was that moment.

This last year has seen me at my worst and I have released that anchor holding me back, and broken that chain of lazy snivel-dibble and dis-ease of my own making. But the fallen Angels had other ideas. They rocked up in a pirate ship called "Corona" as they cracked open a bottle of the delicate golden light-tasting beer. Fuck, they were having a laugh at my expense. Five weeks later, I emerged from my sweat-drenched sheets of dreary despair, disassociated from my own putrid sick room.

One's health is one of the greatest gifts of the gods and I treasure it dearly as I drink my ionized water, oxygenated health juice and erase that dis-ease right out of my hair... singing along with the radio to *Fairytale of New York*.

"You're a bum
You're a punk
You're an old slut on junk
Lying there almost dead on a drip in that bed"

Ha Ha, the Pogues know how to cheer up a room!

This year has had so many contradictions, contrary conundrums of catastrophic encounters, the balance and imbalance, the reflections of duality, what goes up must come down with that fallen crazy angel.

Fuck, he was smoking an illegal Cuban cigar.

I was carving out a space for my heart to let love in, then threw it out with the old bath water, then made it camp at the bottom of my garden in a festival tent, then opened the door, dashed the feelings, hid under the stairs, denied my heart, fooled my head, jumped off the edge of the cliffs of reason to swim in the warm embrace of a breeze thru the beaches of Southern Cornwall.

I may have jumped a little fast from sickness to love encounters of the very first kind. But in this moment, I became aware that the time might be running out on this OG Tuesday's Wild Writers night, and I wanted to let you know that I am not all doom and gloom, hmmmm... but disaster and mishaps make for a more humorous story, or so I believe, or a laugh at the juxtaposition of my own torment, from the deathbed... ok I'm exaggerating, from my sickbed to a bed of red roses with love songs running thru my head.

The Pogues sum it up best...

"I could have been someone
Well so could anyone
You took my dreams from me
When I first found you
I kept them with me babe
I put them with my own
Can't make it all alone
I've built my dreams around you"

This year has been one of the wildest, funnest, sickest, freakiest and most adventurous – but I think all my years are blending into one. As I can't quite differentiate between one and another one, before then and now or next. . . .

Do you think maybe I held onto the joint earlier, for just a little too long, my friend? Here, you have it now, my lovely, and pass me the cocaine-D-stained & tarnished mirror.
I'm kidding; I'm kidding; I'm. . . kidding. . . .

I just like to dance around in my underwear and sing out loud to the wackiest Christmas songs. . . .

And as the Pogues sum it up so beautifully, I shall bow out to their shout out to us, reprobates all, and to all a good night.

"You scumbag, you maggot
You cheap lousy faggot
Happy Christmas your arse
I pray God it's our last"

Bah humbug. . . . Here have some too much, too sweet, too yellow eggnog sugar waves of sea sickness as we gyrate on the dance floor to out-of-tune guitars wishing for a better start next year. Well, this has been fun, let's do it again, shall we. . . NOT?

"And the bells were ringing out
For Christmas day"

BEGIN

JESSE GROS

Mama used to say,
"All things must come to an end, so that new things can begin."
It's true.
Winter is coming for all of us.
We will lose our leaves.
And we will return in spring.

Breathe in the fresh air.
No mask.
Only smiles.
For the first time in two years, my daughter no longer has to wear a mask at
school. She said to me, "Daddy, I got to see my friend's face for the first time!!
She has a really nice smile." I have noticed how much happier I am now that
masks are off. I love people. I love hugs. I love smiles.
I feel new beginnings on the horizon.
Hope is intoxicating.
It's so light.
Light-bright-blue translucence... floating.

Spring is here.
I can't wait to commune with the desert.
To hear the coyotes howl at the moon.
To howl with them.

One with the stars... small and humble, yet free.
Hello cosmos.
Hello.

Billions of tiny white little dots...
Each its own planet, star or solar system.

Turn off your phone.
It's hard to commune with the Divine when the lights are on.

Fire touches the soul in a primal way.
The stars tell us there is always another way.

So, my dear, make your way…
Through the valley of ego death into a hopeful space.

Let the past die with the changing of the seasons.
And make way for the new.

You never know when your life is going to change… forever.
One smile.
One opportunity.
One right turn, instead of a left… and there you are.
It all changes, just like that.

David Whyte has something to say about this:

"In that first hardly noticed moment in which you wake,
coming back to this life from the other
more secret, moveable and frighteningly honest world
where everything began,
there is a small opening into the new day
which closes the moment you begin your plans.

What you can plan is too small for you to live.
What you can live wholeheartedly will make plans enough
for the vitality hidden in your sleep.

To be human is to become visible
while carrying what is hidden as a gift to others.
To remember the other world in this world
is to live in your true inheritance…

…Now, looking through the slanting light of the morning window
toward the mountain presence of everything that can be

what urgency calls you to your one love?
What shape waits in the seed of you
to grow and spread its branches
against a future sky?"

WHAT'S NEXT FOR ME?

PEDRO PEDRO

What isn't next for me? It wasn't that long ago I felt trapped in a cage of self-imposed limitations. Like an animal from the wild that suddenly finds himself on display at a zoo behind rusty bars. My friends and family all saying: *"Rob, get out of that cage. What's wrong with you? It smells!"*

We find comfortable cages in our narratives. It's human. But I was the world champion of that for a bit. I could come up with all sorts of reasons for how I ended up there for the better part of three years — the pandemic being one of them. But they are just excuses. I could have opened the gate. I had the key. I was perfectly aware of the delicate house of narratives I built for myself. Somehow, it was more comfortable to live inside my stories and deal with the constant state of emotional discomfort than to open the cage and deal with the emotional pain waiting for me on the other side.

It's wild how a long-term relationship impacted so many aspects of my life. For the last two years I had trouble even asking myself, "what's next for me?" I didn't want to, to be honest, because I was afraid of the answer. And now, suddenly, there are no limitations, self-imposed or otherwise. For the first time in my life, at age forty-seven, I find myself 100% unconstrained. The sky is the limit. I've never had this much freedom before. In fact, it's overwhelming at times. And confusing. I've spent the majority of my life working my way up from one level to the next, from one challenge to the next, not quite knowing where the end is. Now, somehow, I don't see that next level. There are no gorillas throwing boulders at me, or an abyss I have to jump over. I look around me and the world looks lush and flat. The sun is shining.

What's next for me? I have no idea, but I'm getting used to not knowing. I think I need to live in this space for a while. Just see what comes, feel into things, take my time. I get to play another kind of game, one where I don't have to work my way through an obstacle course. A game where the level I am on gives me more time than I'm used to — or at least the timer is hidden. There is nothing I need to find, shoot down, or unlock. I've never played this game before.

What's next for me? A period of self-reflection, a chance to explore a different side of life and an opportunity to make space for love.

WHAT WAITS TO BLOOM?
ERIKA BRIDGES

Do you think the snow is a long-lost friend of the flower? Star-crossed lovers, even? Is the flower that friend that all of Snow's acquaintances talk about, but the snow never gets to meet? The fox mentions, "This one time with Flower…" or the Cricket says, "My friend Flower told me about this place we should go…" But it's one of those things where it doesn't line up and the two of them never get to meet? Snow belongs to the winter universe and Flower to the spring. In the very brief transition period they may meet, but chances are small, and things could even be hostile.

In life, we have seasons. When I am in my own wintering, it feels like I may never get the chance to see flowers bloom again. I forget their smell, their touch, and it feels out of reach to hold them again. I have to remember, there is no spring without winter. Winter is the earth's preparation for spring. It's when all the work is really done. The real work of resting, recharging and allowing things to decay, to clear, to absorb, to end, so new things can begin again.

There are so many notes we can take from nature. The earth never feels bad for wintering. Winter doesn't wish it were spring or summer or fall. In fact, it's quite comfortable in its corner of the year. It understands what it is. Existing is enough. My obaachan always used to remind us of this. When we would fight over things, she would say, "Do you think the sun resents the moon because it gets to play with the stars?" or "Do the stars resent the sky because it gets to hug the sea?"

Our answer was always, "Well, of course not, no." To which she would respond, "Well then, enough." And it was.

Instead of wishing I wasn't wintering and yearning to see the flowers, I have to remember that flowers don't just pop up magically in the spring. The seeds were planted long before. I have to let old things die and use that energy to grow something new. I must now sit and decide what I think needs to die to free up resources to let my spring flowers grow.

Spring brings new life, new love, and partnership. Energy is neither created nor destroyed. There is no birth without death. Last year's flowers must decay to fuel the soil for next year's blooms, the death of the maiden to become the mother and so on.

Flowers are the ultimate phoenix, completely comfortable with living and dying each passing year. The Sakura (cherry blossom trees) have a couple weeks a year in full bloom, but you don't see them holding on too tightly. With each gentle breeze, they release their beautiful flowers to the earth, each with a destiny of death to become life the following spring.

The Sakura has wisdom for me: She doesn't make plans. She blooms on her own schedule. She doesn't change how she looks to satisfy others. She doesn't feel rushed to show up when it's convenient for others. She doesn't feel self-conscious if people stare. She receives compliments well. She doesn't fight the seasons. She does what feels right and when she's done, she welcomes winter as confidently as she would spring.

May we all hold things as gently as the Sakura holds her flowers and welcome our many winters as easily as the sun bows to the moon for every sunset.

CYCLES OF CREATION
JESSICA ARONOFF

I go through cycles of creation, creating and creativity, creating through writing, drawing, painting, crafting, collaging. Sometimes a lot. Sometimes rarely. Sometimes not at all. I don't like those not-at-all times.

Lately it is writing. Every day. Because I am a writer. I said so yesterday. Without hedging. Without qualifying. Without self-deprecating. I just said, "I am a writer." And it is true. It is a fact.

People come to my house and say, "I didn't know you were an artist." That is a title I have a harder time owning as mine. But I suppose it is true, too.

It goes in cycles, waves; I go in cycles, waves. Recently not a lot of art. I miss it. I miss my hands covered in clay or paint. I miss the quieting of my mind. I miss the focus, the absorption, the way it envelops and holds me, or perhaps more accurately, the way it holds the rest of the world at a slight, quiet distance, like a bubble of peace surrounding me.

I create love too. Gathering the courage to reach out. Inviting in love. Expressing desire for closeness, intimacy, laughter, connection. That cycle sometimes feels more like a roller coaster. Sometimes, like the familiar loop, I walk in my neighborhood.

Everything is cyclical. I feel stress and it passes. I feel settled and that passes, too. I feel afraid and it passes. I feel shrouded in clouds and rain and those also pass.

People often invoke the expression, "And this, too, shall pass," as a reassurance that things will get better. But I think that is missing the point. The real point is that all things will pass. It isn't about eternal optimism; it is a recognition of impermanence, of ephemerality. And this applies equally to the good, the bad, the joyful, the sorrowful, the frightening, the thrilling, the boring, the confusing, the peaceful. Life itself – living, aliveness.

I think some people find this understanding of "And this, too, shall pass" to be unsettling. But for me it is the opposite. It is comforting. It is a reminder that I am so small and the universe is so large. Look at the starry night sky! How can the fact that I tripped on the edge of the rug in a crowded room at a party matter at all? (That didn't happen, by the way.) I'm just talking about the metaphorical trips on the rug. Those do happen. Daily. And they don't even register on the light meter of life. How could they, when the stars shine so bright? When the planets and the moon appear to be shining, but really it is the sun's light they are reflecting? I mean, come on! That is magic. That is worthy of registering and remembering.

And yet, even that is impermanent.

So it's probably OK that my own acts of creation are cyclical. The universe and I are in sync that way.

What is creation, anyway? I create every day – the song I make up to sing to the dog about the sweetness of his face and the smelliness of his breath, the email to my board of directors sharing updates and inspiration, the salad made from lettuce I grew myself, the texts with my mom and sister that leave us all crying with laughter.

The first time I learned that forest fires are not inherently bad – that in fact, they are a necessary part of the ecosystem's cycle of creation – my mind was blown. It overwhelmed me. It is just so beautiful. The fires only become a problem when human behavior – settlement, building, and especially suppression – gets in the way of the natural cycle. The years and years of trying to suppress fires is what ultimately makes them so destructive and deadly when they – inevitably – do what they were designed to do.

I have tried to suppress the fires, too. How foolish. How futile. How potentially deadly.

The wise me knows better: Allow the fire cycle to move through, and marvel at the seedlings left behind, suddenly receiving the sunlight they need to grow.

A NEW SEASON IS UPON US
IONA RUSSELL

Hey, I have been expecting you.

A new season is upon us. Put down your bags; they look quite heavy.

It is time to dance thru the portal of incandescent transcendence. . . .

Oh wait, I hear it now.

Shhh. . . listen. . . .

Ahhh. . . there it is at last, do you hear it?
The rhythm drumming thru your veins and reverberating across the stars of
expansion.
I have it on very good authority that we are all just star stuff, you know. . . .
It's time to shed that outdated, false narrative and that moldy, weather-beaten
snakeskin. It smells quite putrid, those lies of misbegotten-forgotten-dreams
with tarnished distractions, teasing you and misleading you down the path of
fakery and mockery, false prophets, false kings and false queens.

Consider this your best one yet, but only if. . . .

Only if you should choose to stop that childish corruption, competition, and
corporate greed, and jeeeze. . . you need to seriously ditch those dark-night-
cigar-laden-distorted conversations.

Have you not felt it yet?
There's just no music in those dank bar rooms. It's an untuned barbaric
patriarchy screeching ballad. And it hurts the heart. No one wins.
It's checkmate, baby.
So, just pause a moment right here. . . and look. . . look from this elevated
perspective, above the murky musky smog, and away from the din of decadence.

Out there – on the horizon within your soul, what do you feel...?

Breathe deeply and nourish yourself with this clean, effervescent air.

Breathe deeply and listen... listen deeper still....

Ahhh... there it is. Can you hear it, too?

Can you hear your exquisite symphony pulsating thru the web of life, connecting and connected to the spell of life? Weaving into the tapestry of the natural rhythms, this is your symphony. It's the universal sweet symphony of truth and wisdom.

This is THE last dance should you choose it. To live dancing as one great wave of consciousness, dancing on the stuff that stars are made of.

WALKING THE CAMINO
MARTHA JEFFERS

I walked, for what seemed hours, in the blazing sun. My traveler's hat guarding my face and the pole in my hand leading me forward step-by-step. Alone, meandering along a mountain path, I came across a lovely meadow peppered with wildflowers of lavender and pink and I sat down to rest.

I'd been on the road for two weeks at this point, traversing the ancient Camino. I'd met people coming and going, each *peregrino* (pilgrim) carrying their own reason for stepping onto this ancient path to Santiago. For some pilgrims it was a form of retreat from the shadows of their lives. For others, it was a spiritual journey for deeper connection to the God of the Universe.

As I sat in the meadow, I began to reflect on what I was experiencing, not only in that very moment, but also on my own reason for taking this journey. I lay quietly on my tattered blanket. I watched the clouds form visions and wondered about this simple yet brave-hearted journey I had undertaken. Was it really a religious quest? Or was this framed as a way to test my desire for adventures? How does one truly decide at any given moment what this life is all about?

Falling into further inquiry, my imagination flickered through a life review. I began to relive grand moments of awakening and not-so-grand events filled with trauma. Thoughts came spilling out like beaded mantras on a mile long *rosario* (rosary), chanting the sorrow-filled mysteries and divine epiphanies of my then sixty-three-year-old body.

In that sacred moment, the mountain top gave way to moments of clarity. It beckoned me to enter the ritual of purification and release.

I began to lift each doubt, fear, condemnation, wrongdoing, and guilt out from those places inside that held them captive. The invisible strings tied to each mental belief controlling me became visible.

One by one, I clipped the puppet strings. Each surgical cut gave way to grief. Each dismantling snip gave way to greater freedom. Fanned by a gentle breeze and touched by a gentle rain, I laid to rest a part of me that day. As the heavens' holy water bathed me, I felt intimately held by the Mother. The God of the Universe was blessing me, as Love's balm healed all those places inside that so profoundly ached.

REBEL OR NOT, HERE I COME

SHERI KELSEY

I've never been a rebel, but I've certainly had plenty of cause. Too much cause, perhaps, that it caused me to tame myself at a very young age. I think I was afraid. Afraid of my wild, afraid of what it could do, afraid of what others would think, so:

I held in those screams.
I ate that judgment.
I muffled my voice.
I held back.
I stifled my nature.
I walked on eggshells.
I gave too much of myself.
I people-pleased like a motherfucker.
And now – now I want to say FUCK THAT.
The need to break open far outweighs the fear. The need to laugh and sing and dance around alone, naked in my living room, exceeds any judgment. The idea of jumping into a car and driving across the country just because I can is reason enough.

Eating Apple Jacks for dinner will always be a good idea to me.
I will never feel too old for a theme party – I know this deeply.
Martini glasses can, and should, be used for mashed potatoes and mac n' cheese.
Sunsets will always speak directly to my heart.

And where the hell am I going with this?

Honestly, I don't know; I don't want to know. I want to be surprised. Surprised by life. Throwing caution, routines and fear-based 'what-ifs' to the wind. Because what if the best things in life haven't happened yet? What if the best is truly yet to come – new discoveries about life, about ourselves, talents hidden within interests we don't know we have – are living just on the other side of our fear, nestled beneath our wildness?

What if I move back to New York City and stay until I'm 85?
What if I visit Santa Fe for the first time, love it so much and buy a house there?
What if I move to LA instead of back to San Francisco post-pandemic?
What would happen? Who will I meet? Who will I become?

What if I scrap what I think I should write about and write something else?

What if I'm an artist and haven't embraced that fully yet?
What if I howl at the moon?
What if I learn Reiki?
What if I also hike the PCT?
What if I let go? Then let go some more?
Then, even more than that?
What if I never stop letting my imagination run?

What if I love myself for being wild-hearted without an ounce of hesitation?

Maybe I'll have another glass of wine.
Maybe I'll buy yet another pair of nude shoes.
Maybe I'll punch the punching bag without crying.
Maybe I'll do nothing at all.

But those are my decisions to make, my thoughts to consider, my life to create. So, rebel or not, here I come. Ready and willing to explore every bit of faint (or massive) wild-heartedness within me. And for no other reason than BECAUSE I CAN.

TAKING THE RISK

ASTRID VINEYARD HERBICH

The original meaning of the Greek word *apocalypse* is "the uncovering."

It seems to me that in a lot of ways safety, comfort, our preciously-mundane everyday routines cover our true selves up like a down blanket, irresistibly enticing us to stay asleep.

But once that blanket is pulled off the bed, we lie bare-naked in the cold, shivering, struggling to maintain our sense of self.

When we have no one to tell us who we are, no one's expectations to fulfill,
When we have no job to hand us our sense of purpose,
No home to come home to,
When our bodies are falling apart around us,
Who are we then?

What is left of us?

We all shed our skin a couple of times in our lives.
Some more than others, some deliberately, some by necessity or force of man or nature.

At one point in our lives we all find ourselves standing alone and naked, stripped of everything we thought we were, like a newborn baby, having to decide: Who am I going to be now?

Ending a relationship can feel that way.
Moving to a different place, a different country.
Losing a parent.
Letting a career go and deciding to do something completely different,
Because you suddenly know:

I am not this person anymore.
I have, without barely even noticing, shed that skin and left that life, person, or place behind me.

And now here I stand.
Naked and alone, cold and terrified.

And free. Absolutely free.

Not even my clothes tell me who I am right now.
No shade of lipstick to guide the way.
No stilettos, sneakers, or army boots to scream at the world: "This is who I am!"
The only thing I hold in my hands right now is a question.

I have no shoes, but I am still a dancer.
I can dance barefoot and naked in the rain.

My painter's eye ignites with the colors of the sunset, clouds scattered across the sky like coarse, deliberate brushstrokes of a genius.

I am the breather of this breath.
I have a voice and I can fill the night sky with my song and make the moon sway and swoon.

I have these hands.
I can build a sandcastle out of dreams and let the ocean carry it away to another world.
Maybe it will take me along to live in Atlantis and ride on dolphins.

I have feet and I can start walking.
I'll just choose a direction and who knows where I'll end up and who I'll meet along the way.

I have this grateful heart.
Joyfully beating its own rhythm, full of love and longing, constantly opening and closing, willing to break and blunder and bloom.

I have this soul. I have a soul.
My precious undying, fearless self,
patiently guiding and comforting me, every step of the way,
always reaching out to me as I stumble through this life like a child just
learning how to walk.

And unfailingly, every time I think I've found my strut, I'm walking my walk,
I'm surefooted and safe, graceful and accomplished,
There comes another storm on the horizon to strip me of my delusions.
Wind and hail, rain and thunder, shaking me to the bones, blowing me over,
blowing me away, bringing me to my knees,
And once again I have to admit:
I know nothing.

I am standing, cold and shivering, bare-naked in the rain.

And I have choices to make.

And only one question in my heart:

Who am I now?

INTO THE NIGHT
JESSE GROS

I will not go quietly into the night.
I will not go without a fight.
The owls hoot a warning.
The wind howls.
The leopards prowl the edges.

The frogs croak and ribbit down by the creek.

The night is full of sounds.
And so am I.

My mind is full of thoughts.
And so is yours.

Quiet is not something we humans seem to do very well.
David Whyte says, "The reason we are so afraid of silence. . . we fear our surface personalities will not survive the encounter."

Our Egos
The "I" we speak of,
Will not go quietly into the night.
They will not go without a fight.
Always.
Everyday.

"Your ego never wants to do your soul's work.
The good news is, it doesn't have to." - Ron Hulnick

Check your ego at the door. . . if you can.
Let's see what the other side has to say about this life.

Dear heart, what do you think?
Should I stay or should I go?
Should I turn left or turn right?

My ego chimes in, "I will not go without a fight!"

Oh, dear ego, don't worry.
With a little breath, we will put you to sleep.
Will a little dance or a yoga class, we will sweep you right off your feet.
Like the gentle caring of a first love.
You won't even know what happened.

Sometimes kind, sometimes useful ego, you won't need to fight.
Let's do that, shall we?

Shall we dance together?
Shall we waltz around the room, stepping on each other's feet?
I'll do it.
I'll show you how.
No, no, you will do it.
You show me how.
Oh, forget it.
Let's just do it together.
Making it up as we go.
Boisterous and lively.
Let's not go quietly into the night.

Besides, that's no fun anyway. . . right?

--

I will not go quietly into the night,
He said on the eve of his destruction.
I will yell in defiance.
I am still here!!!
You have not struck me down!

As if. . . his demise was caused by some outside force.

As if. . . God,
As if. . . nature wanted him dead.

Oh no, young man. . . .
Look down in that pool of flat water and you will see with whom you need
to converse.
Look down in that pool of murky water, struggling to see your own reflection,
and ask yourself, how did we get here?
And when you get the answer,
Say to yourself,
I am sorry.

--

I will not go quietly into the night, said my heart. I will not let my romantic
notions of life fade into the straight lines of adulthood. While it is true. . .
some of our juvenile hallucinations must die, many of our romantic notions
are actually meant to live,
And be reborn again and again.

Cynicism is just a fad.
It's just a scab over a wounded heart.
It serves no real value but to block us from our unresolved pain.

There is always hope.
There is always a shot at redemption.

So, dear heart.
Hold my hand.
I will be kind to you.
I will listen.

And together, let's believe once more.

MEET THE CONTRIBUTORS

Members of the Wild Hearted Writers' Circle

Astrid Vineyard Herbich
Astrid is a dedicated Yogi performer, piano teacher and vocal coach. A lover and doer of all things artistic, she grew up in Austria, running around in the halls of an old castle, hiding out and reading lots and lots of books. The writing circle affectionately calls her "Shakespeare's Girlfriend." She has a sneaking suspicion that she was born about 300 years too late, because writing long letters in flourished cursive makes so much more sense than online dating.

Martha Jeffers
An elder badass, at 77 years old, she's fully engaged in life, exploring, adventuring, growing her coaching practice and showing all of us youngsters what we have to look forward to. Her writing is influenced by her love of God, her Colombian heritage, the joy of her children, grandchildren, and family tribe. marthajeffers.com

Sheri Kelsey
A biotech marketer on a self-proclaimed adult time-out in Los Angeles. You can find her laughing at herself while performing stand-up, providing sound baths, and writing in coffee shops, sipping an oat latte. She is the author of *Layers and Waves*.

Motty Kenigsberg
A life coach, workshop host, father and entrepreneur. Mott is on a journey of authentic living, helping people live their truth. He was born in Israel and grew up in the Hasidic side of Brooklyn, NY. Mottykenigsberg.com

Iona Russell

Based in Scotland, where magic and mystery come alive, she gracefully connects the gritty 'real world' with her wandering spirit, blurring the veil between tearful experiences, mythical masquerades and the ramble-bamble-cosmic-flow of curiosity and playfulness. Come and sip some puzzle tea as we explore what's possible. ionarussell.com

Betsy Gibson

Betsy is a happily-married entrepreneur, traveler and mother of 6 children, 13 grandchildren and 4 great-grandchildren. Betsy lives in her left brain most of the time, but wanders over to the other side through her music, painting and writing.

Patrick Faulwetter

Conceptual Designer and writer based in Los Angeles. artstation.com/patrickfaulwetter

Arminda Lindsay

Arminda is a keen observer of human nature, a poet and a spiritual psychologist. Her writing draws on her former life as a devout Mormon and subsequent journey through abuse, divorce, and single motherhood. Arminda consciously creates peace in her own life while transforming the lives of her clients. Writing: allarminda.com - Coaching: armindalindsay.com

Mick Breitenstein

He has been a bartender, stuntman, a film producer, director and martial arts instructor. "I washed dishes in my father's restaurant, installed roofs with my grandfather, but at my core I am a storyteller. Now that life has slowed down a bit and I no longer jump off buildings for a living, I make time to write, take long walks with my dog Bear and tend to the home I share with the love of my life in theCatskill Mountains."

Anj Bee

Anj Bee, otherwise known by her literary pirate alter ego, Rani Shetani, is a California-born, London denizen of Indian, Pakistani, and Scottish descent, raised in every religion except Judaism before the age of 13. An artist and data nerd at heart, she is most passionate about using data and culture to drive positive social change.

Sara Falugo

Yogi and founder of the Yoga Nest in Venice, CA, she is a medicine woman and a lover of life, passing her days on the big island of Hawaii.

Lauryn Hill

Lauryn is an Artist, Career Coach, and Creative Strategist who lives in Los Angeles, CA. She teaches workshops to help creatives who are seeking clarity, confidence, and direction in their work. Her writing is a form of personal therapy; she channels whimsical, humorous, and dark imagery to portray the many sides of our complex human experience. www.curatedsplash.com

Janelle Nelson

Mother of one and former pastor's kid.

Janelle is a licensed Marriage & Family Therapist who specializes in trauma and codependency. She is the Clinical Director & Founder of the *Wholeness Collective Therapy Group*. She is also the EMDR advisor and partnering therapist for *To Be Magnetic* - a neural psychology-based manifestation company. www.wholenesscollectivetherapy.com

Pamela Henry

Pamela is a Lego-loving, book-reading, art-collecting, sneaker-wearing, crystal junkie, life adventurer who considers the awesome relationship she has with her grown sons to be her greatest accomplishment in life.

Jessica Aronoff

Jessica is a Los Angeles-based mom, nonprofit CEO, truth-teller, play-seeker, curiosity-follower, and pursuer of adventure, connection, and belly laughs.

We hope the voices of our Wild Hearted Writers' Circle have touched your heart, ignited your spirit, and connected you with your own journey of personal growth. Whether you found yourself laughing at moments of shared joy, shedding tears or feeling the warmth of inspiration from the depths of these stories and poetry, our ultimate goal has been to connect you with yourself.

As you turn the final page of this book, we encourage you to be courageous on your own journey of personal growth and healing, just as our writers have. The path to self-discovery is a lifelong pursuit, with many paths to enlightenment. (Or at least more fun and less suffering.)

Maybe your journey includes joining our community of Wild Hearted writers or joining us on a spiritual adventure retreat in the Andes. Or maybe it's time to finally start meditating. Are you ready to commit to writing your book, as many of our members have?

May the stories you've encountered here be a stepping stone in your own exploration, a testament to the resilience of the human heart, and a source of inspiration to continue your path of growth and healing. As you venture forth, remember that you are not alone; you are part of a vast, interconnected community of explorers, all on their own extraordinary journeys toward authenticity, joy, and wholeness.

Love,

Jesse & the Wild Hearted writers

JOIN US ON A RETREAT!

www.jessegros.com

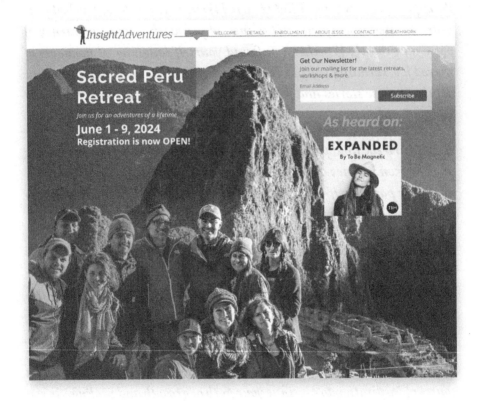

ACKNOWLEDGMENTS

Alexandria Zech for your love, support, design & graphics. Adam Donshik for a beautiful layout. Tiffany Peterson and Liza Garcia for your fine proofing work. Arminda Lindsay for your final edit. Peter Engler for your keen eye for detail. Devon for being a lovely source of joy in my life.

Lupin Grainne for the cover photo.

A special thank you to all of the members of the Wild Hearted Writers' Circle!

ABOUT JESSE GROS

Jesse Gros is a Life Coach, retreat leader, and LEGO artist.

Jesse brings tools and wisdom from spirituality to professionals experiencing the "midlife opportunity" of finding greater meaning and purpose in their lives.

Jesse has a Masters in Spiritual Psychology, is a TED speaker coach, and is the author of *Your Wild & Precious Life* and *My Life Coach Wears a Tutu*.

He is also passionate about mentoring **coaches, therapists and healers** to up-level their practices to be more profitable, authentic, and fun — something he knows a lot about. In the midst of the 2009 recession, Jesse walked away from his lucrative professional career to follow his own calling and create a thriving coaching and international retreat business.

He lives in Marina Del Rey with his family. When he's not coaching, guiding retreats and leading the Wild Hearted Writers' Circles, you will find him building large-scale, custom LEGO models. @westside_lego_daddy

JOIN THE
Wild Hearted™ Writers' Group

Wild Hearted™ is a supportive, playful, and provocative writers' space where we free ourselves from personal critique and allow our innate gifts to shine. Through the process of writing and receiving direct feedback, we build our self-confidence, foster intimacy, and create a fertile environment to grow both as writers and people.

Join us for eight weeks as we gather together online. Through guided meditations, creative prompts, and breathwork, you will experience a dynamic and uplifting online environment to move through resistance and express your inner life with the pen.

jessegros.com

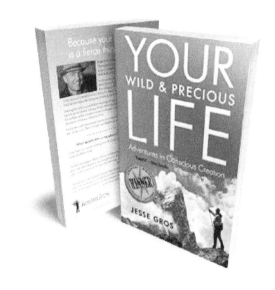

"Powerful." — Steve Chandler

Jesse takes us on his journey of walking away from Corporate America, traveling the world and creating his own path. A mind-opening tour of a heart-centered life, filled with joy, compassion, and self-discovery.

Also by Jesse Gros

All Books Available on Amazon

Gigi says,

"WOOF, WOOF, WILL YOU WRITE US AN AMAZON REVIEW?"

jessegros.com

Made in the USA
Monee, IL
20 January 2024

51671255R00164